066023

F
Mon

DISCARD

DEMCO

066023

William

Monahan

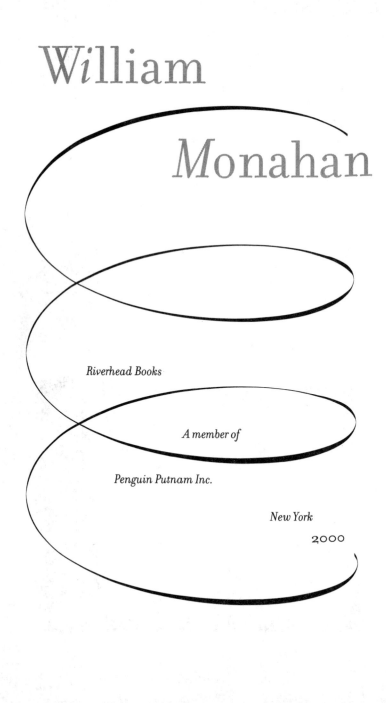

Riverhead Books

A member of

Penguin Putnam Inc.

New York

2000

Light House

A Trifle

Riverhead Books
a member of
Penguin Putnam Inc.
375 Hudson Street
New York, NY 10014

Library of Congress Cataloging-in-Publication Data

Monahan, William.
    Light house / William Monahan
      p.   cm.
    ISBN 1-57322-158-9
    1. Artists—New England—Fiction.   2. Gangsters—Florida—
Fiction   3. New England—Fiction.   4. Florida—Fiction.
I. Title.
PS3563.O5162L54   2000   99-086047
813'.6—dc21

Printed in the United States of America
10   9 8 7 6 5 4 3 2 1

Book design by Judith Stagnitto Abbate / Abbate Design

For Cinder

Contents

Light
House

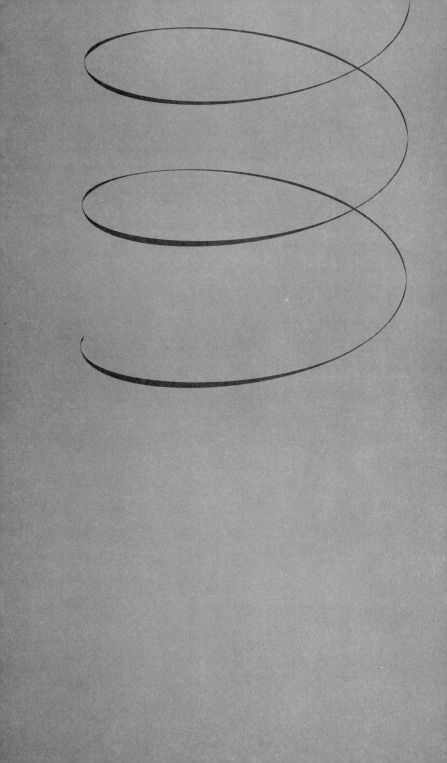

Chapter 1

In Which a Potential Hero
Becomes a Very Savage Criminal

TIM PICASSO did not know whether such a thing as
a criminal mind existed, but if it did, he did not, so far as he
knew, have one. Like everyone else, though, he thought
from time to time of doing something roughly unlawful.
His fantasies of crime took a specifically cinematic direction. At the age of sixteen he had entertained an enthusi-
asm for international art theft. In Tim's view, being an

international art thief mainly involved suavely upending condesas (film ones, not the real ones with warts and mantillas), poisoning Alsatians (whatever they were), and breaking into castles in Spain to the accompaniment of an ominous John Barry score. Obviously, this was more of a fantasy about being in a 1960s film than it was about making off with the loot. Obviously, Tim was not a criminal. When he was at art school in Boston a few years later, though, he realized that he could not go into a museum without trying to figure out ways to infiltrate the place at night—with daring, ropes, and nobody hurt—to make off with somber Rembrandts, insolent Picassos, exorbitant van Goghs. Then, after having sold the paintings (wherever, of course, one sold a painting), Tim would . . . well, he'd do what international art thieves did, which was drive around in sports cars, wearing sunglasses, smoking cigarettes, and stopping at interesting places for lunch. His actual criminal experience consisted of this: at the age of five, a large-headed child with a solemn disposition, he stole a piece of penny candy—a Squirrel Nut—from a village store. Hiding around the corner, Tim unwrapped the candy and then found himself unable to eat it. He returned the item ("You little bastard," said the nice old man who ran the store), and was dragged into a park and beaten up by his cousins.

The fact is that Tim was an intensely moral person, though without being annoyingly messianic. He had never stolen anything, really, and he never told lies, which, as far as Tim could tell, everyone else did almost constantly. He had an abnormal predisposition for integrity, which in general did him very little good. In his public high school, he was at first popular, the way good-looking people always are—even, or especially, if they are bastards—but he befriended several flinching math spastics, started reading esoteric paperbacks, and was subsequently martyred. At art school he spoke his mind respectfully and intelligently, which is the last thing anybody wants from someone with a highly developed critical faculty. Tim was often in hot water with the faculty for having naively asked Socratic questions at inappropriate moments.

On top of being actively unfair to others, Tim was immensely talented as an artist. This was a kind of brutal and involuntary unfairness, like being good-looking, or being genetically the best pole-vaulter in the world, which meant that quite a lot of people hated him automatically anyway. Tim could produce very carelessly in almost any medium a kind of undeniable artistic success that other people could not seem to accomplish with any amount of effort in a single medium. This was certainly undemocratic, and perhaps it was supernatural. Therefore, Tim had to be discouraged in various ways, for the good of Society. When he applied for a postgraduate grant to teach painting in Italy, it was pointed out to him by Dr. Locarno that Tim's paintings at the time (which were delusively representational and reminiscent of Vermeer) were aesthetically interesting, but artistically invalid.

"I beg your pardon?" asked Tim.

Dr. Locarno had an upright shock of hair and appeared to be undergoing electrocution for sex murder. He glanced at Tim, coughed unnecessarily, and sorted through some papers. "I don't know exactly what I mean," he said. "I realize you've had some success . . . some beginnings of commercial success. Rather unusual for an undergraduate."

"Yes, I'm the only one who can paint."

"Shocking," said another member of the board. "This is why you get nothing."

"You've sold paintings," said Dr. Locarno, who was still giving his own paintings away to friends.

"Shakespeare made money," said Tim, with his usual destructive candor. "But doesn't mean he didn't need Southampton's guineas."

There was an interval in which the members of the board tried to figure out what Shakespeare had to do with Italians on Long Island.

"We're disturbed by your application essay. 'Beauty'? 'Truth'? What in God's name are the Keatsian verities? When I looked at your proposal I thought I had gone mad. Where's your compassion for the Human Condition? That's what we want. Where's the Human Condition?"

"In every painting, sir, I think."

"Well, we want it overt. Have a look at Ms. Rindle's *Oppression* series. That's Art. Let me tell you something, Picasso. Art isn't about talent anymore. It's about Sincerity."

"I see," said Tim.

"I'm afraid you're not dispossessed enough. I'm sorry. We have limited funds."

Tim spent the next several months in his studio apartment in Boston, brooding, painting, starving. He spent all his money on slides and postage, and got a show together in New York City. But the gallery caught fire, and the only result was that Tim unknowingly exerted influence upon—

i.e., was ripped off by—a number of more established painters, while getting nothing himself, and running the insane but very common artistic risk of being ultimately perceived to have plagiarized the people who are actually your plagiarists.

In desperation, Tim wasted a few months trying to write a novel (he was also good at that), but then, like any respectable member of his generation, he succumbed to profound inanition and despair. Tim had great powers of impassivity (very common in the "insipid" hero of the traditional bildungsroman), and being a New Englander, he went fairly respectably about the business of disintegration.

One day, coming out of a bookstore in Cambridge (he had just sold the last of his books, and was wondering vaguely how much he could get for his overcoat), Tim ran into his friend Andrew Spine, an Australian reputed to be rich, who for some reason posed as a student of art history at Harvard. The two men went into a bar.

"Graduate?" asked Andrew Spine.

"What?" asked Tim.

"Go forth into the infinite world to make one's mark."

"No."

"I didn't, either." Andrew stuffed peanuts into his mouth. "Never do. That's not the point of it, for a gentleman."

"Vexilla regis prodeunt," said Tim, who was extremely well-read.

"What's up, then?" asked Andrew, who wasn't.

"Nothing. I don't have any money. I think I'm going to die."

"Have you tried to get a job?"

"No," Tim said.

"Know how to sail?"

"Not really."

"Are you prone to motion sickness, or a closet homo-sexual?"

"No."

"Ever been down the Islands?"

"As a matter of fact I haven't," said Tim.

A week later he was on the island of Tortilla, sitting on his duffel bag at the edge of a dock in a palm-thatched slum, sketching listlessly, while Andrew Spine made fur-tive phone calls and talked to some people who were lurk-ing in an adjacent bar. It was very unclear to Tim, who was wearing dark glasses, what, precisely, was going on. A po-liceman with a machine gun asked him, successfully, for spare change. He did a few watercolor sketches, and in-stantly sold one to a Norwegian couple, who then tried to take him back to their hotel. When the tourists had been discouraged, Tim lit a cigarette and brooded.

However brilliant visual art is, he thought, and had for months been thinking, it is a kind of basket-weaving. It had belatedly occurred to Tim that *any* of the traditional media, late century, were very medium mediums. It was possible that there was no longer any honor to be obtained in the arts. As far as painting was concerned, surely it de-noted insufficiency as a man to be overly interested in lay-ers of pigment, and the production of artifacts that may have been better than most, but which were nevertheless trivial. Tim stared with Elsinorean dubiety at the fifty dollars the Norwegian tourists had paid him for an undifficult thing that had cost him nothing and in which he was not even interested.

This troublesome facility aside, what if he didn't make it as a painter, anyway? What if, through no fault of his own, he *didn't* become a brooding maestro of international fame, with a French farmhouse and galaxies of esoteric mistresses? He imagined himself at sixty, crippled, climbing in and out of a wrecked panel van at Yosemite, handing out sad cards and surviving on the thin sales of books titled *Watercolor Witchcraft* or *Chiaroscuro Made Easy*. He'd submit arduous, deeply informed masterworks to juries of craftsy widows and socialist crackheads like Dr. Locarno, in the thin hope of winning $125 every once in a while, and then finally die in the gutter, coughing pitifully. "Artists" like that existed. Tim had seen them.

Worse than that, he might even end up teaching. He imagined himself wandering inebriate around faculty parties (Tim foresaw the post-Romantic wreckage he could easily become, because he *was* a Romantic) and ultimately offing himself with a swan dive from the ersatz campanile of a midwestern college when it was impossible to live with himself anymore. But there was no getting out of being an artist. Tim knew one great and salvatory truth: that art, like sincerity, took care of itself. Tim would be an artist even if he was reduced to the interior of his own mind. Dr. Locarno could be an artist only if he got a lot of people to agree to call him one, and had a lot of theories and positions and a particular kind of beard.

Andrew Spine suddenly reappeared, striding through

the hard Caribbean sunlight. "Look, I might as well tell you now," he said. "This isn't an ordinary boat delivery. In fact, few of them are. The yacht was not only stolen from Venezuela, it's full of cocaine."

"Oh," said Tim.

"Have any problems with that?"

"Yes, I think I do."

"No worries," said Andrew. "They bought it off the Coast Guard."

Tim couldn't see where he had much choice in the matter, and they went to sea without incident. Tim never did learn where the cocaine was hidden. Andrew talked cryptically of false masts and hollow keels. Tim had his suspicions about the fact that in the galley the lockers contained hundreds of cans of cheaply labeled Chinese water chestnuts. ("They get left," said Andrew. "People don't eat them.") Tim didn't worry about it. He was content to read a buckled copy of *Hamlet* which he'd found in the cabin, and to steer a course fairly ably on his watches. Mainly he stayed out of Andrew's way when he was doing anything complicated, which is the soul of seamanship.

Andrew Spine was a very good sailor, having been a yacht racer for years. But he was Australian, and therefore perpetually drunk, with, furthermore, an alarming tendency to piss off the rail without holding on to any part of the boat. Two days out of Key West, Tim came up on deck, squinting in the marine sunlight, to find the yacht rolling in a heavy ground swell, the sails luffing, and Andrew nowhere to be seen. Tim looked everywhere, but Andrew was demonstrably gone. All that was left of him (apart from a wallet crammed with credit cards) was a solitary deck shoe lying pathetically on its side and an empty rum bottle rolling around in the cockpit.

Tim lowered the sails, started the auxiliary diesel, and turned the yacht north.

Chapter 2

The Excellent Jesus Castro

Two days later, Tim motored single-handedly into a lagoon below a ramshackle marina on a flyblown key, where he was met by several paranoid Hispanic gunmen and a gentleman named Jesus Castro, who assumed benignly that Tim had murdered Andrew Spine at sea. He paid Tim double, in the genuine spirit of professional admiration. Tim, having failed three times to explain what had actually happened, glumly stuffed the twenty thousand dollars into his duffel, and under some duress accompanied Mr. Castro to Miami.

At length, over piña coladas by his shark pool, Mr. Castro revealed that there was another job for Tim, as Andrew Spine, being dead, was unavailable. Although Tim could hardly penetrate Mr. Castro's syntax at first, it was eventually clear that Tim was being asked to deliver some sort of vehicle (crammed with cocaine, apparently, like every other vehicle, object, or person in Jesus Castro's immediate sphere of influence) to Boston. The pay for this would be ten thousand dollars. If Tim worked out, he could have Andrew's job as Jesus Castro's New England distributor, though obviously the condition in which Tim had delivered the sailboat (he'd hit a reef off the Tortugas, and rammed the gas dock at Key West) unfortunately precluded Tim's being considered for further maritime assignments.

Tim replied that criminal employment was, in his case, not a very good idea.

Mr. Castro argued the opposite charmingly. He assured Tim that he would be absolutely safe. Indeed, in accepting the job, Tim would be very much safer than he would be if he refused. Business had many exigencies, explained Mr. Castro, some of them not so pleasant as others. Tim saw that this might be (extraordinarily) the case, and therefore agreed to drive the vehicle to Boston.

So it came about that Tim was Jesus Castro's guest for a few macabre days, during which he was kept under wraps eating avocado dip and reading spy thrillers in a rudimentary pastel mansion in South Beach. He consoled himself with the fact that he was, at least, no longer broke. Finally, he was driven by night to Sarasota, where in a plot of wasteland near the clown college he was given the keys to a gigantic, underpowered Winnebago recreational vehicle with Michigan plates, and a Beretta pistol. Tim looked at the pistol with cogent alarm.

The camper stood beneath a stand of blighted palms. It was positively plastered with Police Benevolent Association stickers, advertisements for retirement parks, and various forms of Christianity. Jesus Castro walked Tim to the camper, a heavy arm around his shoulders. Tim was wincing in the morning sunlight and walking very reluctantly.

"Take it easy," said Jesus Castro. "Have fun. Stay some nice place. And whatever you do, don' let no one look in the fucking refrigerator. In Boston they give you a bag. Don' look in the bag or I fucking kill you."

"All right," said Tim uncertainly, determined to do the best he could.

"I see you in Boston four fie day. Kay?"

"You'll kill me if I don't go?" asked Tim, just to be sure.

"Sí," said Jesus Castro.

Three days later, Tim was in Boston. He drove the camper across the Fort Point Channel into South Boston. He left it locked up, as directed, on a particular street. Then, in the din and smoke of an Irish émigré pub called the Cup and Drum, he handed the keys to the bartender, said, "Jesus loves you," and left without having a drink. He popped by his apartment and gave his landlady a thousand dollars to ship his paintings to a hotel in Como, Italy. Then he took a cab to the Copley Plaza, and registered as Andrew Spine. He had Andrew's wallet: there was no sense in not using his credit cards, and a good deal of sense in not surfacing as himself at any point during the proceedings. He ordered a steak and a bottle of Bordeaux from room service, ate heartily, and then fell soundly asleep in the king-sized bed.

The next day, precisely at twelve noon, he went downstairs to the hotel bar, and took a seat in some sort of half-assed palm garden, ordered coffee from a crippled waitress, and waited (meanwhile realizing that he'd forgotten his pistol upstairs) for Mr. Castro's money to appear. Two Irishmen arrived, who treated him with a certain reverence. The IRA was bad news (even the Boston fundraising branch), but Jesus Castro, apparently, was infinitely worse. "How der yer got in whitter man?" asked one of the Irishmen under his breath, and when Tim said, "I'm sorry, I don't know what you just said," the Irishman said, "Fookin' West Brit Boston branch ennui, bastard," and tried to climb over the table at him.

When the Irishmen eventually finished their pints and departed, it was without the large aluminum briefcase they had brought in. Tim retrieved it from beneath the table and carried it fairly coolly, he thought, up to his room. The message light was flashing on the telephone. Tim had been downstairs a little longer than he had been instructed to be, and had missed his statutory twelve-thirty call to Miami. He sat on the bed with Mr. Castro's phone number in hand, reviewing in his mind what he had been instructed to do. When he had remembered all of it, in bright and extraordinary detail, he decided to do something else instead.

He took the butter knife that had come with his room-service breakfast, and used it to break the locks on the briefcase, revealing a pot of clotted cream from Cork (evidently a gesture of goodwill toward Mr. Castro) and a million and a half dollars, half of it in ultranegotiable bearer bonds, and half of it in hundred-dollar bills. Tim looked at one of the banknotes and wondered, not for the first time, how it was that Ben Franklin still managed to seem extremely urbane for an American, even though he had been dead for two hundred years. He was a good man to have on money, though, when you were having ideas about it. Benjamin Franklin, like the Mona Lisa, looked as if he were twelve steps ahead of you, and not particularly in a good way, either.

Tim transferred the money and securities into his cracked leather duffel. He sat down on the bed, picked up the telephone, and using both Andrew Spine's credit card and a passable Australian accent, purchased a first-class plane ticket to Sydney, a first-class ticket to Singapore, and a bus ticket to Mexico City, all in the name of Andrew Spine. As a final touch, he called a florist and sent a dozen roses, in Andrew's name, to Jesus Castro in Miami. He then shaved the beard he had grown at sea, clumsily inspected the load of his Beretta, and left the hotel without checking out. On a windy corner in the February twilight (there was rumor of a storm), after having made reasonably sure that he hadn't been followed, he gave all of Andrew's credit cards, gold and platinum, to a vagrant who had asked for a quarter. Then, pleased with himself, he flipped Andrew's empty wallet into a trash barrel, and after a moment's reflection, wandered toward North Station. Why North Station? It was a sudden decision—like a decision in art—not rationally explicable, but making perfect and obvious sense. Tim bought a ticket for the train that at that moment was being called; and so he walked down the platform and boarded a train for Tyburn, Massachusetts, where he had never been before.

Rain lashed the cloudy windows and streamed on the

smoking hull of the commuter train. Tim sat very comfort-
ably, waiting to depart for Tyburn. He did not, perhaps,
have a criminal mind, but he had a very good mind, and it
seemed to him that if one did not wish to be tracked down
and executed—which was obviously his basic goal—the best
thing to do would be to act unreasonably or according to
whim (that word which Emerson said should be carved
above each and every door). Being whimsical—or protean—
was not difficult for Tim, especially when he had a million
and a half dollars to be whimsical or protean with. On the
whole, he figured, there wasn't much to fear. Jesus Castro
didn't even know his name, and most likely did not keep up
with avant-garde art journals. Tim Picasso, with a million
and a half dollars, a working knowledge of Western Civilization, a stupendous amount of unfocused talent, and the
vague intention to reside in Italy, opened a paperback, and
read:

> *Though spiteful Fortune turned her wheele*
> *To staye the Sphere of Destinye*
> *Yet dooth this sphere resist that wheele*
> *And fleeyeth all fortune's villanye*
> *The heauens to fortune are not thralle*
> *These Spheres furmount Dame Fortune's alle.*

Tim became absorbed in his book, and forgot immediately about the immediate past. Which was unwise, because
staring at the back of his head was an extremely expensive
private detective named César Pilosi, who had been engaged by Jesus Castro in Miami.

Chapter 3

Some Intelligence of the Abominable Mr. Glowery

M r. Glowery (who had also boarded the train, wearing a damp toggle coat and dragging a huge suitcase full of complimentary copies of his autobiographical novel *My Early Life*) did not know if such a thing as an original mind existed. But if such a thing as an original mind existed, he did not, so far as he knew—which is not to say that he admitted it—have one. Yet in no way did he consider this an insuperable defect. As an artist, Mr. Glowery was a late-century pragmatist of the New York school, interested in temporal approbation and appearances, as opposed to immortality or accomplishment. This was the philosophical lay of his Manhattan career as a literary person, and a sensible policy it had proved to be. Mother Glowery may have raised one architect, the man known as the Tri-State Cannibal, an Oedipal wreck in the insurance business, and a housewife susceptible to religion, but she had not raised any original people.

Mr. Glowery deviated from the character of his generation in many ways, but in no way so much as in that he was a *tireless worker*. Not for him that "slacker" thing, lying around with all this enormous talent and not doing anything with it because the world was a piece of excrement. He was focused, and indefatigable. He *had* to be focused, and indefatigable: he was, frankly, not much of an artist, and all he had therefore to sell was a kind of redundancy—

which is a tricky thing to sell in any business. But he had tackled this dilemma smartly and was a diligent expander of his own reputation. Mr. Glowery sucked acquaintance. He wrote congratulatory notes to people who could help him. If Mr. Glowery had felt it necessary to slam a knife into the back of a literary rival whose full proud sail outclassed Mr. Glowery's leaking coracle (a bedraggled craft that wandered here and there, patrolling Manhattan erratically for canapés and sinecures), he would have done it without hesitation, and his fiction, like his conversation, was mainly à clef, filled with disfigured enemies.

Like most evil, self-interested people, Mr. Glowery thought (it may actually be a form of innocence) that everyone else was as evil and self-interested as he was, and that no matter what he did to harm other people, he was merely protecting himself intelligently against enemies as obsessive as himself. Mr. Glowery really believed that everyone did this sort of thing constantly.

He was haunted by the specter of Talent and on some days he really believed he had it—but mainly he forgot about it, and focused indefatigably on self-promotion. He gave readings regularly. His metier at the moment was the garish millennial confessio. Mr. Glowery, you see, was a geek. If fucking a live chicken in Tompkins Square Park would have gotten him two lines of notice in the *Aristocrat*, he would have done it twice, and then have been shattered and vengeful when no one asked him to have drinks.

It did not end there, of course. Mr. Glowery did have a book out. *My Early Life* (a novel à clef about a New York writer who *really* wanted to be one) stood at number 67,325 in the Amazon sales rankings, and in an attempt to chivvy the book into cybersales Mr. Glowery would borrow other people's e-mail accounts and write in with reviews comparing Mr. Glowery to F. Scott Fitzgerald, Montaigne, Lady Murasaki, Apuleius, Homer, and so forth, managing inevitably to make unfavorable mention of living writers whom Mr. Glowery considered rivals. Writing was business, after all, and Mr. Glowery knew that business depended on advertising.

Although in theory every person who had ever picked up a pen was his enemy, he did have one great enemy, the reclusive and manic-depressive dipsomaniac *John Wong*, a former classmate who in contrast to Mr. Glowery did nothing to promote himself, yet at random intervals would offhandedly publish a novel and instantly win film contracts and fiction prizes. The obsessive tracking of such progress kept Mr. Glowery perpetually on the verge of nervous breakdown. It was a secret matter related to *John Wong* that had caused Mr. Glowery to board the train to Tyburn.

Mr. Wong, Mr. Glowery knew, had started out (with a considerable and unforgivable leg up, in Mr. Glowery's opinion) in a literary magazine called *Up Periscope*, which was run by a then itinerant English professor, Dr. Menelaus Eggman. While doing a little research with an eye to planting a negative tidbit in the newspaper about his great enemy *Mr. Wong* (who had recently become famous enough to be mentioned in gossip columns), Mr. Glowery had struck gold. Another embittered Manhattan writer had revealed to Mr. Glowery a suspicion ("Well, it's more than a suspicion") that *Mr. Wong*, whose novel *Hamlet, Prince of Denmark* stood at number 4 on the Amazon charts, was a monster of literary fraud. According to Mr. Glowery's informant, *Wong*'s first novel, the startling *Actual Modern Fiction*, had been utterly rewritten by his early mentor and college instructor Professor Eggman.

This information electrified Mr. Glowery. He mentioned it to everyone he could. But for such a particle of information, mere *mention* was an insufficient response— like having a hydrogen bomb, and detonating it out in the middle of a field. But Mr. Glowery, perusing the *New York Times* Sunday book review at a coffee shop one morning, in his usual shattered way, had a stroke of unbelievable luck. Professor Eggman, inveterate compiler of unnecessary anthologies, had a book out titled *The Best Short Stories in the History of the World.* Professor Eggman, also, was that very next weekend running a seminar, advertised as follows:

PROFESSIONAL FICTION WORKSHOP

Prof. Menelaus G. Eggman, BA, MA, MFA, Ph.D.
Novelist and Educator
Author, Enameled Balls:
The Modernist Imagery of Mary Butts
Author, Here I Am, *a novel*
Editor, The Best Short Stories in the History of the World
Editor Emeritus, Asymptote to Asymptote Quarterly Review
Founding Editor, Up Periscope Quarterly Magazine

Will hold a two-day intensive seminar
in PROFESSIONAL WRITING
to be held at
THE ADMIRAL BENBOW INN
Tyburn, Massachusetts

Mr. Glowery, as a sometime journalist and book re-
viewer, had a certain level of access to anyone in the world
of letters with anything to sell. Professor Eggman obviously—and usually—did. It would be possible therefore,
on a journalistic pretext, for Mr. Glowery to interview
Menelaus Eggman, ostensibly about his book, then slowly
work around to the subject of the hideous *John Wong*, whose
very existence, as we've mentioned, profoundly tortured
Mr. Glowery and, frankly, a lot of people like him.

Mr. Glowery positively leaped to the pay telephone and
called Professor Eggman's publicist. Within five minutes
he was speaking to Professor Eggman personally. Professor
Eggman would be delighted to be interviewed by Mr. Glowery; he would in fact be more than delighted to have Mr.
Glowery participate in the workshop, as Mr. Glowery con-
stituted that most encouraging spectacle to workshoppers—a writer who had actually gotten paid for something
he'd written. So this trip was to Mr. Glowery an intoxicating
mix of vanity and revenge. He sat seraphically on the Tyburn train, with a pocket full of reading flyers and a suitcase full of presigned copies of *My Early Life*, in which a
character much like Mr. Glowery continually outscored
a character much like *John Wong* not only in literature, conversation, and the bedroom, but in every conceivable field
of human endeavor.

Mr. Glowery, mucus glistening in the stubble beneath
his nose, with five dollars to his name, his entire worldview
irised down until he could see nothing but *John Wong* running around being successful specifically to torment him,
was psychologically very much a man on the edge—even be-

fore he glanced across the train compartment and saw a dark-haired, blue-eyed young man of artistic demeanor reading a paperback copy of *Wong*'s so-called critical triumph *Hamlet*, an audacious rewriting of an apparently preexistent story about an indecisive prince.

"I know that man," said Mr. Glowery.

"You do?" asked Tim Picasso.

"In New York."

"*John Wong* doesn't live in New York. He hates New York."

"I'm a writer in New York." Mr. Glowery was reaching for a card advertising his book, reading, self—whatever it was that he had left to market. His ass probably.

"I think I'd know where *John Wong* lives," said Tim vaguely.

"An interesting thing about *John Wong*," Mr. Glowery went on, "is that he was completely rewritten by Professor Menelaus Eggman."

"No he wasn't," said Tim.

"How would you know anything about *John Wong* or his relations to Professor Eggman?" asked Mr. Glowery.

"I should hope I know something about him," said Tim.

"Why, because you've read that book?" said Mr. Glowery, sneering.

"No, because he's my brother-in-law."

Mr. Glowery vomited in the aisle of the train.

Chapter 4

George and Magdalene at Home

The northeast gale began with a deceptively slow rain in the almost balmy air that lingered after a mild, blustery winter afternoon. The wind built steadily, though, and by nine o'clock the barometer was plummeting and the wind was blowing twenty knots. In an old inn on a headland above the Atlantic (where Professor Eggman lay snoring in a bed on the third floor, dreaming in the third person), the innkeeper, George Hawthorne, stood looking out of the seaward windows of the parlor, trying to get a glimpse of the defunct lighthouse, which was situated on a rocky island three-quarters of a mile to sea. The lighthouse was invisible. This was uncommon, but the night was unusually black. George could not see anything beyond his own dismayed reflection in the glass.

"I can't see a light out there," said George.

"So what," said Magdalene.

Magdalene, who was knitting, was his wife.

"There was a light earlier," said George. "I hope he didn't try to make it in."

"He wouldn't," said Magdalene.

"He drinks out there, you know." George looked significantly at his wife.

She looked back at him with the expression of disdain she usually directed at evidence of his hypocrisy. Which was in this case unfair. George was merely stating a fact:

Mr. Briscoe *did* drink quite a lot, not only out at the light-house but everywhere else as well. George was genuinely concerned.

"He drinks," repeated George. "I'm not saying that I don't drink, Magdalene, I'm saying that *he* does. Too."

"And he sleeps out there when it's rough," said Magdalene. "He sleeps out there when it's not as rough as this, even."

"That barge he has isn't seaworthy. He made it himself, you know, out of scrap metal."

"George, he's drunk out there, sitting by a fire eating beans from a can or something. He's in paradise, and we're doing okay, too, George, because he's out there doing those things, and not doing them here. All we have to worry about is that shitty professor."

"I ought to call the Coast Guard," said George. "Just as a precaution."

Tall, lank-haired, bespectacled, George went shambling off toward the telephone in the lobby, wearing what Magdalene more or less privately thought of as his cuckold's cardigan. She heard his affected patrician voice conveying a stream of convoluted information into the phone. Magdalene dubiously continued knitting. She had turned thirty-five, she was married to an innkeeper who had just spent an entire winter's grocery money on liquor for guests who didn't drink (she saw his plan, there), and worst of all, she was knitting. Her life was bogus. She had terrific tits, of course, but that didn't solve everything.

The tenantless main part of the house, where Magdalene sat, was underheated and drafty. A mouse dawdled insolently along the baseboard, then disappeared beneath a radiator. Magdalene bit her hand, and started crying. George came back into the room. Magdalene looked up, winsomely, as if she had expected someone else—saw George—and then, still smiling, resisted a dazzling impulse to kill her husband with a hatchet.

"They were very nice about it," said George, uneasily. "The Coast Guard. They said we ought to wait and see."

"No shit."

"They were very nice about it."

"Everybody hates you, George. They hate you instantly."

"Oh, that's an awful thing to say."

"I bet they weren't nice. At all."

George said nothing. Magdalene was triumphant.

"They seemed to be busy, of course," said George, "but they said they'd try to raise him on the radio."

"Who?" demanded Magdalene.

"Mr. Briscoe. At the lighthouse."

George blundered about for a moment as usual, running his hand through his lank hair and nervously eyeing and narrowly avoiding the drinks table. He finally picked up a tremendously overdue library book on shipwrecks, which he had been reading, or pretending to read, or looking at, for what seemed like months. The unreturned library book was the locus of some recent dementia. It was George's subconscious plan to be arrested for something idiotic and be thus relieved of responsibility for his life for long enough to really sit down and write some cracking poetry. He had an idea that prison might work. He'd tried everything else. Recently he had timidly defaced an encyclopedia, too, but no one had arrested him.

The wind had begun to howl seriously, and the fire roared in the updraft. George sat down in a sprung club chair and opened his book. He had gone to Harvard, and to Oxford as a Rhodes scholar, but he read very slowly, tracing sentences with his finger, and moving his lips. It made Magdalene crazy. He sat there, hunched over his book, humming to himself, moving his finger and his lips. He came across a plate of *The Raft of the Medusa*.

"You know, if anything terrible did happen to Mr. Briscoe, Magdalene, we don't even know his next of kin."

This was not absolutely true: Mr. Briscoe had mentioned a sister in Virginia.

"You *want* something terrible to happen." Magdalene looked up from her knitting.

"What an awful thing to say."

"It's true. You lie in wait for something terrible to happen so that you can pretend to be competent. Which you aren't. At all."

"Bullshit."

"You sit there with that book of shipwrecks. I know what you want. You want a shipwreck to happen, so that people will pay attention to you when you interrupt their conversations in the coffee shop."

This indictment was followed by silence, during which George (as he always did when anyone said anything true about him) smiled with a half-smile of hurt and disbelief. He had just opened his mouth to object, when a most unexpected thing happened: the doorbell rang.

Magdalene stuck herself with a knitting needle. George leaped to his feet as if he had heard a gunshot. The bell rang again. The bell itself, over the door to the lobby, simultaneously buzzed and cracked, throwing blue sparks and emitting a wisp of smoke from the antediluvian wiring. George stood staring.

"Someone's at the door, George."

"Christ," George said. He smoothed his hair.

"It's a drowned sailor. He's coming for you, George."

"Those become gulls," said George.

He coughed, buttoned his cuckold's cardigan, smoothed his hair again, and galloped off toward the front door. Magdalene tensed and listened. She would have been satisfied to hear a piercing scream from George . . . but there was only a murmur of civil male voices, dampened by the wind, and then the sound of the door (which was warped and had to be kicked) closing with a thud and a second tinkle of its little bell. Footsteps came along the hall toward the sitting room.

George could never simply bring a guest to a room. No, the first thing he had to do whenever he met anybody was to pretend that he had a normal marriage. Magdalene stood, anticipating that she had to be gracious, belatedly aware that she was wearing mismatched athletic socks. George admitted a diffident young man into the room—proudly, as if he had accomplished something of definitive value.

The young man was slightly shell-shocked, and soaked with rain, but he was handsome, with the most piercing blue eyes, and a good deal of natural charm. Tim stood there staring with alarm at Magdalene, who had a face like a Quattrocento Madonna, and to be fair, tits like rockets.

"How do you do," said Tim.

"Enchantée," said Magdalene unpleasantly.

Chapter 5

Some Adventures of Mr. Glowery in Tyburn

Mr. Glowery, in the familiar embrace of a mental breakdown, had decided to not go immediately to the Admiral Benbow Inn. His mind was utterly blown—as yours might be—by the fact that he had, while thinking about his great enemy—while actually on the way to *investigate and expose* his great enemy—been superlatively trumped, beyond any possibility of seemly recovery. Whoever was at him—*John Wong*, the Universe, the people on television who were always talking about him secretly—something bad had definitely happened. Vomiting and chuckling to himself in the malodorous bathroom of the speeding train, Mr. Glowery, cramming pills into his mouth, had found himself torn between two glittering options in the world of insanity. On the one hand, there was rocking back and forth silently in a padded room somewhere. On the other, there was obviously an opportunity for a spiritual crisis of enormous dimensions which quite obviously would end with either the receipt of holy orders or a shooting spree. If *John Wong*, previously understood to be The Rival Poet, *was* actually God, as now seemed to be the case, the game was up.

After stumbling off the train at Tyburn and watching the train's lights disappear in the direction of Waxport, Mr. Glowery peered around a corner of the station building and spied upon Tim Picasso. The bastard was leafing through

yellow pages in a lighted booth. He laughed openly at something he read. Then, what Mr. Glowery regarded as classi-
cally *John Wong*–esque disregard for the work of others, the
object of Mr. Glowery's beady observation ripped a sheet
out of the phone book, made a call, and then settled in, still
chuckling, to wait in an adjacent bus shelter.

Mr. Glowery, sleet dripping from his face, desperately
needed a drink—if ever a sailor needed rum, it was he—and
he noticed a bar across the street, but decided to keep an
eye on Tim for a while. Episodes of a fantastical sort had
never left Mr. Glowery unmolested. He was frequently
convinced that the people at the next table in a restaurant
knew perfectly well who he was, and were making coded
references to either him, or *John Wong*. Obviously Mr.
Glowery had a problem, occasionally answerable with fash-
ionable medications, but they weren't working very well.
And just as Tim got into a car marked "Tyburn Taxi," Mr.
Glowery was approached with some urgency by a person he
took to be a giant homosexual.

"Have you got a car?" the apparent sodomite inquired,
grabbing Mr. Glowery roughly by the arm.

"Hotels exist," said Mr. Glowery, in a louche and practiced tone.

César Pilosi stared at him openmouthed. Mr. Pilosi
wore a soaked loden hat which was too small for his head,
and held not only the waterlogged remains of the yellow
pages from which Tim had torn a page, but also a *duplicate*
directory, from which he, Mr. Pilosi, proposed to obtain
the exact page that was missing from the other one. He was
an extremely resourceful private detective, as well as an ex-

pensive one. You might think that gangsters always send their own boys around to do the sort of thing that Mr. Pilosi was doing, the trailing and the finding and the beating and the killing: not true. Jesus Castro's boys could not read English, and the great proportion of them, as Jesus Castro often had sadly to admit, could not find their own bums with a mirror. They were hard men, certainly: they were also illiterates living in a foreign country.

"Did *he* send you?" demanded Mr. Pilosi, wondering suddenly if *that* was why Mr. Glowery had been peering around the corner at The Subject.

"Who?" asked Mr. Glowery.

"Jesus."

Mr. Glowery was convinced then that he had certainly lost his mind.

"I don't *know*," said Mr. Glowery.

"Are you from Miami?"

Mr. Glowery brightened and reached for his flyers. "No. I'm a novelist. In New York. I give readings."

"You're not a dick?" interrupted Mr. Pilosi.

Mr. Glowery considered, rain dripping from his face.

"Well. As an artist you can't always be nice to people."

Mr. Pilosi seized Mr. Glowery by the lapels and slammed him eight or nine times into the cinder-block wall of the station, while screaming, "I work for Jesus, you know who that is, don't you, you prick," and so forth. Mr. Glowery dropped his obsolete laptop, which smashed, and most of his performance flyers spilled into a tremendous puddle of slush. Mr. Glowery somewhat voluntarily fell down.

"Listen," said Mr. Pilosi, standing over Mr. Glowery and jabbing at him with a finger, "I know who you are, you mick bastard, and I'm telling you from Jesus, and you *know* who that is, that this has nothing to do with the IRA."

"Right," said Mr. Glowery, whose nose was bleeding. He nodded. "Obviously."

"This is not your business. You go anywhere near that guy, or anyone who knows him, I will fucking kill you with this."

"With what?"

Mr. Pilosi produced a gigantic knife.

"Oh my God."

"I want you back on the next train," said Mr. Pilosi.

"I don't have any money," said Mr. Glowery, beginning to cry. He got to his feet. "I'm here for a literary workshop."

He added this as if it were consecutive—as if you could get money at literary workshops, which isn't true at all, either on the spot, or by extension.

"You figure it out."

Mr. Pilosi put his knife back into his coat and headed toward the phone booth.

"You can tell John Wong," said Mr. Glowery, his courage organizing itself as the distance increased between him and Mr. Pilosi, *"that I know his game!"*

Mr. Pilosi, having no idea who *John Wong* was, or why Mr. Glowery was talking about him, pulled out a Taser and shot Mr. Glowery in the neck with it. There was a crack of blue light. As Mr. Glowery was not only standing in a slush puddle, but a grand mal epileptic, the effect was monstrous. He toppled backward into the puddle, foam bubbling horridly from his mouth. Mr. Pilosi crouched beside him and said:

"That's from Jesus, pal, and there's more where that came from." Then he disappeared into the storm.

It took Mr. Glowery a little while to collect his flyers, clean them off as well as he could, and make it across the street into the bar. It was a very rough-looking place, but Mr. Glowery forged ahead, sitting down at the bar, and with his last five dollars he ordered a brandy Alexander. He paid four, tipped one, and then spilled the drink.

"My drink spilled," said Mr. Glowery.

"Tough shit," said the bartender.

Chapter 6

Some Particulars of Mr. Briscoe

Well, there are no other guests, actually," George was saying to Tim Picasso, "which is good for you, though not exactly salubrious from our point of view—except for Professor Eggman, Menelaus Eggman, a rather famous, in the minor sense, homme de lettres—"

Magdalene winced openly at the sound of George's French.

"—who's here doing a fiction workshop. And of course

there's our Mr. Briscoe—Mr. Edward *Coffin* Briscoe—related through his mother to the famous Nantucket whaling family—"

"He's making that up," said Magdalene.

"—who's here working a contract of an interesting kind," George said, persevering. "There's a *lighthouse* out there, you see—"

"I can't see anything," said Tim.

"That's a nor'easter for you," said George excitedly. Unable to indicate the lighthouse itself, he instead indicated a painting of it, which hung over the mantel. It was a terrible oil, executed by George himself, in which the lighthouse (apparently afflicted by Peyronie's disease) rose from testicle-like boulders.

"Jesus," said Tim.

"The lighthouse is an excellent symbol in art, and *for* art," said George. "It's got everything—aspiration, light, mirrors of course . . . it's all done with mirrors . . . and then of course there are the rather obvious Freudian and pre-Freudian implications." George bolted down the last of his whiskey and smashed the glass in the fireplace.

"Yeah, there's Osiris," offered Tim.

"What are you talking about?" asked Magdalene.

"Nothing," said George.

"Fertility symbolism in antiquity as it relates to art," Tim said weirdly.

"The lighthouse doesn't have a light in it, anyway. It's defunct. It's unlit . . . a . . . former lighthouse." George, with a nervous glance at Magdalene, conducted the symphonies of aphasia. "It's . . ."

"Decommissioned?" asked Tim.

"Exactly," said George, looking decommissioned himself.

Magdalene knitted away at her mitten, and looked covertly at Tim.

"It's privately owned," explained George, "which is very rare. Someone bought it—Mr. Briscoe won't tell us who *exactly* stands behind Omphalos Realty Trust—and our Mr. Briscoe, his employee, is turning the lighthouse into a summer home for this person. Whoever it is."

George went to switch on another lamp, and the bulb blew out explosively.

"Wiring," said George dementedly. "Happens all the time. Another whiskey?"

"Yes, thank you."

"Anyway," said George, sounding completely transatlantic and homosexual, neither of which he was, "our hotel is Mr. Briscoe's 'base of operations,' as it were." George hooked his fingers in the air.

" 'As it were,' " said Magdalene.

Tim glanced up and saw Magdalene gazing at him ravenously. Alarmed, he turned back to George, who continued:

"He has a barge, you see, which he made expressly for the job—sort of a landing-craft thing, with a bow that . . ." George made an up-and-down motion, bending both arms from the elbow.

"Drops, yes."

"Yes! And well, he has a backhoe out there, and lumber, concrete, so forth, and blasting equipment. As far as I can tell, he's doing quite a job. Quite a job. He operates out of our cove . . . down there . . . which you can't see, either. Poor Mr. Briscoe's stuck out there now in the nor'easter."

A wave hit the hotel.

"Fuck," said George. He refilled his glass.

"The hotel is *shaking*."

"There's nothing to worry about," said George. "This house has been here since 1801."

This was not exactly true.

"I like storms, anyway," said Tim. "I've always thought I might like nuclear war."

"Yes. And complete societal breakdown," said George excitedly.

"Say what you like about societal breakdown," said Tim, "at least there's something going on."

"You've got that right." George turned to his wife. "Magdalene, would you care to prepare a room for Mr. Picasso? Since I made up Professor Eggman's?"

"Not really, George."

"Right. Excuse me, Mr. Picasso."

George lurched out of the parlor and went upstairs to prepare a bedroom. Tim stood for a moment and listened to the high keening of the wind and the baritone thunder of the surf on the headland. When the windows rattled in a particularly virulent turn of wind, it appeared to satisfy him somehow, and he smiled faintly. He sipped his whiskey, examined a copy of Winslow Homer's *Breezing Up*, and then looked around to find Magdalene staring at him.

"May I ask you something, Mr. Picasso?"

"Yes, of course," said Tim.

"Do I look like the sort of woman who knits?"

Upstairs, George banged cupboard doors. Something smashed.

"I don't know," said Tim. "I did notice that you're knitting a mitten."

"I've been knitting in an attempt to stave off insanity."

Tim sat down warily on the edge of an armchair.

"I'm sure that knitting is an interesting and useful thing."

"It isn't. I've been knitting so I won't go crazy, but I've missed the point, somehow, that knitting in itself is insane."

"I wouldn't know about that," said Tim.

"There are mice here, you know," said Magdalene. "Mice."

Tim looked around at the floor.

"Right this way!" George had reappeared in the doorway. Tim gratefully followed him up the gloomy main stairs of the hotel. The stairwell was papered with a pattern of grandfather clocks.

"So! What do you do, Mr. Picasso?"

"I'm a painter."

"Really? I'm a poet."

"Published?" asked Tim.

"Publication is not the business of poets. You know who said that?"

"Emily Dickinson."

"Absolutely galvanized on opium."

The Easterly Room occupied a seaward corner of the second floor. There were rag rugs on the dark wood floor, a writing desk, a fire in the fine old fireplace, and ship-built bookshelves which actually had readable books in them.

The bed was a large four-poster which sagged agreeably. George kicked a woman's nightgown beneath the bed as Tim dropped his duffel on a Windsor chair in the corner. George looked anxious. He knew that it was a very fine old room, but if someone had told him that it sucked, he would have believed it, because that was what George, wringer of hands, was all about.

"This is the Easterly Room. Our best," he said with an uneasy flourish. "Well. Not exactly our best. Professor Eggman of the University of Massachusetts has our best."

"I should hope so."

"His fiction people aren't staying with us, though." George looked disconsolate. "It's a day seminar. I bought all this liquor, too, and they don't even drink. Can you imagine fiction people who don't drink? I've been mystified all day."

"I'm sorry."

"Not your fault. Can I get you anything?"

"A bottle of whiskey, please."

"At least someone's an artist."

George left Tim alone. The hotel might have had mice, and the bathroom might have been down a crooked (positively hallucinatory) hallway, but it also had fine towels and luxurious complimentary toilet articles. Tim emerged from the bathroom smelling of saffron and lavender. He found that George had left ice, a bottle of Irish, and a siphon of soda. There was also a bill for the extraordinary figure of one hundred dollars, which seemed to be in a woman's hand, and had in fact been jetted in by Magdalene over George's weak objections.

Tim made a whiskey and soda, and sipped it, staring at

his reflection in the mirror above the mantel. "Black Dog," he said, raising his glass to himself, unaware that Magdalene, standing on a chair in the room below, was peering at him (actually, up his bathrobe) through the heating grate. Tim said "Black Dog" because the name of the inn was The Admiral Benbow, which was the only reason he had torn that page out of the phone directory.

"Carve it on every lintel," Tim said, getting into bed: "whim." Then he turned out the lights and lay listening to the storm.

Chapter 7

Townie the Clown

Mr. Glowery was saved from thirst—and with any luck, from sobriety—by a Samaritan in the form of an obese restaurant cook, who identified himself as Archy Lafata and who in addition to his generosity had a pointed bald head and was boiling with working-class pathologies.

"Where you from, there, Cap?" he demanded, drinking.

"I'm a writer in New York," said Mr. Glowery. There was a brief, terrible silence.

"Excuse me," said Archy Lafata.

Mr. Glowery knew that there were going to be problems. He had spoken in a fruity collegiate accent. He downed his drink rapidly in the hope that he could get another one before the class storm broke and he was kicked to death on the floor in a blur of grateful pain. He noticed then, with a burst of ordinate horror, that the bartender was reading *Hamlet, Prince of Denmark* by *John Wong*. Everybody read that thing.

"Why don't you just crucify me now," said Mr. Glowery, who occasionally confused himself with several important persons in history.

"You got a nice place down there in New York there?" asked Archy.

"Yes?" hazarded Mr. Glowery.

This was social suicide: it was also a terrible lie. Mr. Glowery's studio apartment was wretched, infested with brazen roaches better than an inch long. He hadn't paid the rent in five months on the principle (apart from not having any money) that the building had been bought by *John Wong* and was now crammed with surveillance equipment. There was no further question, though, about the extent of *John Wong*'s machinations and malice. Obviously he was God. The only question was whether there was a hell for Mr. Glowery to reign in. If there wasn't, Mr. Glowery was dead meat, or a Trappist making jam.

"Non serviam," said Mr. Glowery weakly to no one in particular.

"You got a nice view of the Park and so forth and so on?" asked Archy.

"Yes indeed," said Mr. Glowery even more suicidally.

"I don't have a nice view," said Archy combatively. "I live in a shithole. What do you say about that?"

"Boy. I don't know."

"You don't know. You don't know?"

"What? Am I supposed to know?" asked Mr. Glowery fearfully.

"Jimmy, give us a couple more over here," said Archy to the bartender. "Back 'em up."

The bartender put down his copy of *Hamlet* and procured four drinks.

"I'm very grateful," said Mr. Glowery.

"Mr. Big Stick Writer in New York, I'm the one with money for drinks, and *I'm* the asshole?"

In a corner of the bar, two fishermen were beating up a man with horn-rimmed eyeglasses who had pulled out a paperback in French.

"I never said you were an asshole."

"Who's the asshole?" demanded Archy.

"*I'm* the asshole," said Mr. Glowery, and seized his second cocktail.

"I ain't saying you are," said Archy charitably. "What kinda stuff you write? Thrillas?"

Mr. Glowery gagged, and some of his cocktail came through his nose.

"Autobiographical literary fiction."

Arch Lafata digested this for a moment.

"Who the fuck are you somebody wants to read that?"

Mr. Glowery thought about this inconclusively.

"I don't have a nice view," said Archy, expansively. "I'm a bum."

Mr. Glowery drank heavily.

"Work my ass off every day," continued Archy, "don't do nothin' to nobody, but I'm a bum. Women? They treat me like I'm a bum. I get dressed up nice, go out, have a few pops, try to make nice conversation and so forth and so on and what have you, and what do I see? My ex-wife there, drinking up my child-support, which I break my fucking back for, and telling everyone don't talk to that guy there in the nice orange shirt, he's a fuckin' bum."

"Archy—for God's sake—Mr. Lafata—"

"Fuckin' bitch ex-fuckin' goddamned wife," shouted Archy, "comes up to me, drunk, down the Rigga last Tuesdey and when I say, 'I'm sorry Sharon, I don't *have* no more money,' she *rips* the gold chain right off my neck, right while I'm talking to this attractive young lady by the cigarette machine." Archy belched. "One thing leads to another and so forth and so on, and all of a sudden, there I am getting thrown down the stairs by the bouncers, and then my ex-fuckin' brother-in-law, who just got out of *Walpole*, he was in there for fuckin' *murda*, beats the shit out of me with a tire iron in the parkin' lot. I already got a broken leg from being thrown down the stairs. I ask you, sir, is that fair."

"Well, it certainly doesn't sound fair," said Mr. Glowery.

"I go to pick up my kid, right? Kid's three years old. I go to pick him up, right, and you know what he says to me? He calls me an asshole. Right to my face, he says, 'Don't touch me, you asshole.' Nice language. His mother, as you can tell, is a classy broad. Kid don't wanna get in the cah. There I am. Finally I gets the kid in the cah, and I say, 'Look, MacLiammoir—"

" 'MacLiammoir Lafata'?"

"Yeah. MacLiammoir. Here's his pictcha. That's his sister Siobhan."

"Is your wife Irish?"

"No, she's a Militello. Father's a fuckin' greasa on a guinea boat. Anyway. I say to the kid, 'Look, you can't talk to me like that, I'm your fatha and I love you.' You know what he says to me? He says, 'You're a no-good rat and you live in a hole.' "

Trembling with rage, Archy glared at Mr. Glowery. "Can you ever see yourself in a situation like that?"

Mr. Glowery, the son of solvent parents, a graduate of degree programs in not one but two Ivy League schools, had always conceived that there was a level beneath which he could not fall. Now, cadging brandy Alexanders off a psychotic cook after having been nearly kicked to death in a slush puddle by someone sent personally by Jesus, he was not sure.

"Increasingly," said Mr. Glowery, and started to cry.

"Hey, calm the fuck down. What are you doing in town, anyway?"

"Looking for a friend."

"*I'm* not your friend," said Archy unnecessarily.

Mr. Glowery gagged on snot.

"You better not be a homo, either, because that's one thing I can't stand. I'd fuckin' pop you as soon as look at you. Anyway, listen. I takes the kid up Boston, right, and we go down the Aquarium, there, to see the seals. 'Look at the seals,' I says to him. Kid don't care for the seals. He's got this big ball of cotton candy, get me, he already lost this giant flounder balloon cost me seven bucks, and now he *hucks* the cotton candy in with the seals. What happens then, you ask me."

"I have *absolutely* no idea." Mr. Glowery grappled his third drink to his lips.

"Fuckin' seal *eats* the cotton candy and the stick it's on, and then starts hacking and puking in the water. Seal's choking on the stick, see, that the cotton candy was on. I thinks, Oh Jesus how much they tag you for a new seal? I don't know what to think. Well, the shit hits the fan. This like lesbian zoologist in this sort of *Daktari* fuckin' safari clothing, which I bet comes in right handy for marine biology in Massachusetts, goes, 'Oh, no! Flippy,' and jumps into the seal tank, and grabs the seal—which the seal don't like. Thing weighs about seven hundred goddamned pounds, right, and it smashes her against the concrete, rolls over her, and fuckin' *bites* her, and there she is, unconscious on the seal platform, blood everywhere, while all the seals, including the one that's choking to death, are going apeshit in the pool. Well, I do what any man would do in the circumstances, and I grabs the kid and makes a run for it. You know what happens to me? I get arrested. You think that's funny?"

"No, no."

"Are you laughing at me?"

"No."

"Better not fucking laugh at me. I'll pop you so hard your teeth will come out of your asshole. That's the kinda guy I am. I take my fences straight."

Mr. Glowery imagined Archy Lafata hunting fox and nearly went mad.

"Anyway, so I gets arrested. My lovely ex-fuckin' bitch

wife comes to Boston and picks the kid up at the police station. She leaves me there. I don't get bail. I'm in jail for two
fuckin' days. I owes the Aquarium not only for the seal's
emergency tracheotomy, but I owe thirty thousand dollars
for the seal itself, which died on the table. I owe doctor bills
for the lesbian, about eight fines for this, that, and the
other thing and so forth and so on, and there's also a charge
for—listen to this—assault and battery on a police officer.
Why that, you ask. Well, I'll tell you. By the seals, I forgot to
mention, there's this fuckin' clown sellin' balloons, which
is where I bought the flounder balloon which the kid lost.
When the kid and I pins out of there, this aforementioned
clown starts chasing me down the Aquarium wharf. I go,
Jesus Christ, what is it with the clown, and like any other
guy would, as you might yourself, I turns around and pops
him."

"You punched a clown?" asked Mr. Glowery, to be sure.

"You got it, Cap. A real fuckin' clown, I shit you not,
with the red nose and big boots and wig and shit. I figure
he's just a regular homo with mental problems who wants
to be a clown. No such luck. The guy's an *off-duty police officer* for the City of Boston. I knock him down, his hat and wig
flies off, right? Clown pulls a *gun*. The clown, let me stress,
at no point identifies himself as a police officer. We wrestle, and what have you. Emmett Kelly there whales the piss
out of me on the sidewalk, pistol-whips me in front of my
kid, knocks out two of my teeth, knee-drops me right in the
chest, bangs my head like twelve times into the sidewalk,
screaming this weird shit I can't understand. One thing
leads to another and so forth and so on, and I lose my visi-
tation. You think that's funny?"

"No."

"You better not think it's funny. Okay then, Cap, what's your story?"

Mr. Glowery was fortified by liquor almost to the point where he felt like a regular guy. He belched. "Well, I'm up here for Professor Menelaus Eggman's Fiction Workshop at a hotel called the Admiral Bend something."

"Admiral Benbow. It's out the back shore."

"I was going to get dirt on *John Wong*—"

The bartender looked up from his copy of *Hamlet*.

"—who, frankly, I've been in the way of stalking, but I was just savagely beaten up a man who claimed to have been sent by Jesus."

"Right."

"Big fucking angel," said Mr. Glowery, belching again, "and he had some sort of electric gun. He shot me in the neck with it. This precipitated a grand mal seizure. Now I have to decide whether I'm going to have to serve *John Wong* (in fact, do substantial penance to him) or, seeing that he is God, which I never planned on, revolt against him in a Dedalian or Luciferian way."

"I fuckin' hate that," said Archy.

"Anyway, I'd be grateful if you could give me a ride to the Fiction Workshop. I don't have any money, but I do have forty copies of my book, which have a substantial dollar value. Well. A dollar value."

"You don't have a cah?" asked Archy.

"No, I'm not even Egyptian. You know, it might be *John Wong* who's making things difficult for you. He interferes with people. He's destroyed my literary career and pays people to not go to my readings. God knows what he's done to you. The clown-beating could have been arranged by anyone. The clown *being a cop* is classic *John Wong.*"

"If the guy's an eef, dude," said Archy Lafata, "I'll fuckin' pop him."

Chapter 8

Marriage Is Fun

He *said,* 'Black Dog.'"
    "Surely—"
    "I heard it clear as a bell. 'Black Dog,' he said, and then he said, 'Whim,' or something, and then he got into bed. Which is *my* bed, by the way, as if you didn't know it. If you think you can get me to sleep with you by giving away my room, George, you have another think coming."
    "Oh, for God's sake, Magdalene. The room is booked. Booked. That's why you don't have your bed. Money. Remember money?"
    There was a long silence.
    "I wish we were in Paris, anyway," said George.
    "Oh, *shut up.*"
    "Remember—"
    "I was drunk."
    "The park—"

"Get your hands off of me, George."

"Magdalene . . ."

"George, just sell this place, okay? Give me half the money and you can go back to England and wear your little cardigan and pretend you're English, which you aren't, and talk like your mouth is full of marbles, and I'll go back to New York, and we'll never see each other again, and be happy."

"Magdalene, I—"

"You know what you are? You're one of those men who are handsome in a boyish, bumbling way for about five minutes when you're twenty-five, and then you turn into a sort of staggering middle-aged monster."

"*Em.*"

"I've wasted my life, George. I studied *dance*. What the *fuck* am I going to do now?"

"Oh, it's going to be fine," said George.

"What is?"

"Everything," said George expansively.

"Shut up. Did he pay you?"

"Who?" asked George.

Magdalene drew a deep breath.

"We'd have a great inn, George, if the lights got shut off and the property was seized. People would come from miles around to climb over the IRS barricades and watch your hand shake as you tried to light candles. Vacation *fucking* City!"

George had been thinking of starting a bumper sticker company in the basement. Obviously, he'd have to divert funds. His pet idea was for a bumper sticker that read "Bills. Can't Pay." George thought a lot of people would buy that one. If they could, of course. "Vacation Fucking City" wasn't a bad one, either. The best was one he had thought of while driving: "State Troopers: Always with the Questions."

"Em, Mr. Picasso is paying for the whole week. He may stay even longer, he said."

"I don't like him," said Magdalene.

"I don't think you get the point of the hotel business."

"Oh, don't I?"

"For instance, *I* don't like Professor Eggman. At all. Nevertheless, I went and bought him peaches, didn't I? He's going to use one for a presentation. He's going to ask people if they dare to eat a peach. And hand them out."

"Why are you crying?"

"There was one for every student. The last thing we need around here, is people disturbing the universe."

"What are you talking about?"

George considered telling Magdalene that she was an idiot.

"Never mind. If you could just exert yourself to be a bit nicer to people."

"I don't want nice, George. You're nice. You know what you are? You're the half-baked product of your own half-assed imagination. That's what *you* are."

"Em, please."

"Look at yourself, George! You've never done anything! You've never worked, and you're not an artist, so don't give me that. I've read what you write. It's garbage, George. You listen to me. You're not avant-garde. You suck."

Magdalene switched off the light. George sat there for a moment in the dark.

"Well, thank you very much, Magdalene. Thanks a lot. Boy."

"I've thought about killing you, George, and making it really hurt."

"That's okay," said George.

"It's hardly the sign of a healthy marriage."

"I can't live without you. Em."

"Oh, for God's sake, George. You've lived without money, you've lived without friends, ambition, a car, or talent of any kind. You live *without basic information*, George. I don't think you've even noticed that you're a failing, forty-year-old innkeeper."

"I'm not."

"You're insane."

"Shhhh. Listen. What was that?"

"It's a nor'easter, George."

"No. It's someone going to the bathroom."

"I hate you."

"Well, why did you marry me?"

"I was drunk," Magdalene began, and then said, "Wait. It rings a bell."

"What?"

"It rang a bell."

"He did?" George started to get out of bed.

"No. 'Black dog.' It's something from somewhere. A movie or something."

The proprietor of the Admiral Benbow lay for a long while in the dark.

"I don't know."

"Of course you don't know. You don't know anything."

"Em, I think that the best thing for us would be to try therapy again."

"He's going back to his room now." Magdalene listened to Tim Picasso's footsteps going along the hall.

"Yes. That's the door to his room."

"Where did he say he was from?"

"I didn't ask."

"Why didn't you ask?"

"Because it's rude."

"You're legally *required* to ask, George."

"Em."

George made a grab for his wife, sexual in nature, and succeeded only in being shoved viciously off his side of the bed, where he crashed into the night table. A lamp flared as it smashed. Magdalene stormed into the bathroom. George was cleaning up broken bits of lamp and cold-cream container, when there was a stately knock on the door.

"Yes?" said George, his glasses askew.

There was a protracted silence, and then the baritone voice of Professor Eggman said plaintively:

"I don't know *where* I am."

George found his bathrobe and went to the door. Professor Eggman was, in daylight, a very large pale man with hair once red, and the breasts and bottom of an extensive Dutchwoman. He was now wearing a sort of see-through linen shift, and being prone to head colds, he slept in, and was therefore wearing (since he was in fact asleep), a sinister-looking balaclava. His eyes stared emptily out of the eyeholes.

"Jesus fucking *Christ*," said George.

"I am what I say I am," said Professor Eggman unexpectedly.

"So you are," said George, and closed the door. He had just thrown the bolt when Professor Eggman knocked again.

"I'm thirsty," he cried.

"We only serve breakfast and tea," shouted George through the door. "You'll have to wait for breakfast. Get some water."

"I am what I say I am," repeated Professor Eggman.

"Call the police," said Magdalene, returning from the bathroom. She looked refreshed by the violence, as usual.

"We can't call the police," said George.

"We could if you had money when you wrote checks." She got back into bed.

"That's not the point," said George. "He's innocent of any wrongdoing, Magdalene. The poor man is afflicted."

"*I'm* afflicted."

"Yes, but he's a somnambulist."

"Guess what I'm doing now," said Professor Eggman unsomnambulistically.

Magdalene leaped out of bed and yanked open the door in a spirit of curiosity and vendetta, just in time to see Professor Eggman—who in truth hadn't been doing anything but revolving on a heel at the head of the stairs—tumble backward down the Edwardian staircase. There was one thud, and then a much louder one and a tinkle of glass. George ran to the top of the stairs, expecting the worst (from the point of view of the uninsured), but he was rewarded with the sight of Professor Eggman marching majestically—in his shift he appeared to be under full sail, like a dhow—into the parlor. Even over the sound of the wind and surf, George could hear the lolloping whicker of the professor's corpulent thighs.

George would have gone back to bed, but when he had ventured into the hallway Magdalene had locked the door behind him. So he steeled himself therefore to his task as innkeeper, and went cautiously downstairs. The wind was shrieking, but the storm wasn't as bad as it could have been—or for that matter, as bad as it was going to be. Glassware was jingling in the china cupboard. George, not wanting to startle Professor Eggman, zipped around through the dining room and peered into the parlor. The professor's large square form was seated bolt upright on a colonial footstool by the crumbling coals of the fallen fire. Obviously, Professor Eggman was asleep. Just as obviously, he had wet his pants—or his shroud—and he held a twist of the drenched front of his garment (George hoped, at least, that this was what it was) clenched in his hand.

George noticed that Professor Eggman, also, in his spare hand, was fetishistically clutching an objet (an object, really, but George was George). George ventured closer. What Professor Eggman was holding was an incredibly racist early-twentieth-century salt shaker in the form of an Afro-Am restaurant chef, which the Professor had evidently found in the pantry, where there was a collection of such hideous relics, which had come with the inn. The white eyes and teeth of the chef glimmered in the dark.

"I am what I say I am," said Professor Eggman, in his lectorial baritone.

"Which is what?" asked George. He poured himself a drink.

"I am the Negro Bakerman."

"Professor Eggman—"

"Now what am I saying and why."

"Sir—"

Professor Eggman, chuckling, began to speak verse:

"Now certes that shall I do
Full snelly as a snail
And I shall tach him to
Full nimbly with a nail."

"Sir—"

"Like glass unto crystal. The brightness, the brightness. And whereas I did not see by the brightness of that light, being led by the hands by my companions, I came across the sea to Rheims."

His voice rose, wobbling, to the stage cry of a geriatric thespian.

"O Menelaus, thou art fallen into a *damnèd* art."

"You're asleep, Professor Eggman," said George, shaking him.

At this point Professor Eggman, without waking up, got to his feet and marched out of the room in as stately a manner as he had entered it. He ascended the stairs like, well, the ghost of somebody's father, passing the dazed Hamlet figure of Tim, who had been woken by the crash of Professor Eggman's body as it went down the stairs.

"I am what I say I am," said Professor Eggman.

Tim watched Professor Eggman out of sight, and then went downstairs. George was standing in the middle of the room with his second drink when Tim entered, yawning.

"Who was that?"

"He teaches"—George swirled the ice in his glass—*"creative writing."*

"Is that why he was wearing a mask?"

"I would. A drink?"

"Usually."

"In the language of dreams, Mr. Picasso, what do you suppose a Negro Bakerman might be?"

Tim thought for a moment. "A shadowy artificer? A marplot? A novelist?"

"Well, that's settled," said George. "As much as anything ever is."

Chapter 9

Breakfast of Cardigans

In the morning the weather was grim, the forecast was worse, and the Fiction People began to cancel early. Professor Eggman hogged the lobby telephone most of the morning, furtively explaining the impossibility of refunds, and then at ten grabbed his hat and departed by cab, on the heels of a mysterious call, leaving George to cope. The telephone still rang off the hook, so George simply unplugged it and went into the sunporch to check on Tim Picasso, who was just back from a walk on the hurricanoed beach and finishing his breakfast.

The sky was the color of a bad oyster, and the rocks below the hotel were flecked with spume. The wind was blowing forty knots, and the gulls, sensibly, had not taken to the air. There was a thirty-foot ground swell, with seas—a different thing from a ground swell (seas go on top of a ground swell)—running up to fifteen feet. This made for waves that were forty-five feet in vertical height. (George had heard this on the radio and imparted it to Tim as if it were an expert personal observation.) Due east from the headland on which the hotel was located, the lighthouse island was now perfectly visible, the white scape of its tower rising above the darkening sea.

George, in a wrecked flannel robe, and the sort of slippers Tim associated with grandfathers and mental patients, his hair awry, peered intently at the lighthouse island through a cloudy opera glass.

"There's Mr. Briscoe now," said George. "I think he's waving something."

Tim, curiosity piqued, took the opera glasses and adjusted them as well as he could to focus on the island. Magnified, he saw a very small granite island, with a protected cove. There was a lifeboat-launching ramp below a ruined stone boathouse, and beside the stone jetty there was some sort of makeshift barge—Mr. Briscoe's landing craft—leaping dangerously in the surf. Above the jetty, broken stone steps ran up the ledges to a turfed area, with a single wind-twisted tree, where there was a stubby, ancient light-house, with a keeper's cottage built alongside it. White spray was cannoning into the air on every side of the island. The gray ledges and boulders gleamed white with frozen spray.

"It's quite old," said Tim, now looking at the light-house itself. A wobbly scrawl on the scape of the tower—the scrawl was not old—resembled the letter S.

"It was erected during Washington's administration," said George. "Imagine that. There was a cannibalism incident on that island in 1623."

"Really."

"The men drew lots. For some reason the cabin boy got the short straw."

"They always do, don't they."

"But what about Mr. Briscoe? Can you see him? What's he doing?"

Tim, redoubling his scan of the island, saw that there was indeed a backhoe out there, which of all things seemed to have been used to dig a hole for a swimming pool. Blast-ing flags fluttered tiny and red against the snow around the scraped-out pit. Quite near the light tower was some sort of newly built shed with a sign on it that read "Explosives." Tim scanned the island again. Although there appeared to be things weirdly written on the rocks, there were no human figures visible.

"I don't see anyone at all."

"But he was just there a moment ago. In the tower. I thought I saw him waving something."

"He's got a fire, anyway. There's smoke coming from the cottage. The man is out there alone?" asked Tim.

"It's very worrisome." George would have liked to have been out there alone. He could write poetry.

"Is that actually a swimming pool?" asked Tim.

"Omphalos Realty Trust spares no expense."

"Apparently not."

"Imagine buying a lighthouse. Do you have any idea what it costs?"

Beside the hotel, which had once been a summer house—but not, Tim guessed, of George's family, despite what had been lightly implied—was a good deep-water cove. It was protected both by the headland itself and by a draggled breakwater of granite slag. Inside the cove was a stone jetty with a sort of picturesque fishing shack just at the end. The jetty itself was covered, not picturesquely, with stacks of masonry and lumber. There was a crane, too, the slack cables of which were dinning in the wind. A scabrous Nova Scotia lobster boat called the *Aphros* was moored in the anchorage, adorned with a hand-lettered sign:

THERE AIN'T NO ELEC. GEAR
ON THIS BOAT. KEEP OFF IT.
SIGND YR. WORSE NIGHTMARE
ED C. BRISCOE

"Mr. Briscoe is a character in the Yankee tradition," George explained. "My wife adores him. She's a New Yorker, you know. Thinks New Englanders are a species of elves."

"They are, aren't they?"

"Not Mr. Briscoe."

The doorbell rang.

"Fiction People!" cried George, and rushed away.

Tim looked back out at the sea through the opera glass. There was no shipping visible, anywhere. The malevolent clouds in the northeast were taking strange pillarlike forms: one looked like a waving nun, another like a man making serious progress on a one-legged camel, and still another like James Joyce in his Latin Quarter hat. Snow was beginning to fly in the slaty air. Tim snapped the opera glass shut and, the coffeepot in the parlor having crapped it, went along to get more coffee, from the supply that had been laid on for the Fiction People in the billiards room.

The billiards room, adjacent to the sunporch, was the most seaward room on the first floor, a gallery-like flag-stoned chamber on a somewhat lower level than the rest of the inn, containing an ornate Victorian billiards table, a fireplace, and an adequate bar. There was also a grim semi-circle of thirty uncomfortable metal chairs arrayed on the flag floor. Someone had thought to put signs on them that read "Reserved." By a fire at the end of the room, a just-arrived Fiction Workshopper, a porcine white woman in a tentlike tribal dress and some sort of African head-wrap, was writing therapeutically in a green marbled notebook. She looked up the moment Tim walked in.

"Are you Mr. Glowery?" she asked rapturously.

"No," said Tim. "Who is Mr. Glowery?"

"He's a brilliant experimental writer from New York. Professor Eggman is very excited that he's coming. He's intensely phallocentric, of course, but his more epiphanic work has such control and sensitivity."

"How could epiphanic work in the short story be experimental?" asked Tim, pouring coffee. "It was new in 1904."

"I think you *are* Mr. Glowery."

"I don't know who he is."

"I'm Saraswati."

"What kind of name is that?" asked Tim.

"It's Sanskrit."

"You don't look Sanskrit."

This was lost on Saraswati.

"Are you in the Fiction Workshop?" asked Saraswati.

"No. I'm an artist."

Saraswati ran into the adjacent bathroom. Tim stood holding his fresh cup of coffee for a moment, and then went back into the main part of the hotel, where he found George in the parlor, wrestling with a capsized samovar.

"It wasn't more Fiction People," said George. "It was a Jehovah's fucking Witness."

"I saw one. I think. A fiction person. In there. Evidently I said something wrong."

"Good. Maybe she'll start drinking."

Magdalene appeared, drinking a cup of tea with the tag hanging out. She had overdressed for the provinces in a cashmere coat and a beret with a feather. She had put on a good deal of makeup and was redolent of some dark, expensive perfume. She smiled frigidly at Tim, and then stared significantly at George. George looked back at her dully for a moment, and then, excruciated, began to address Tim. But Tim had already counted out the money he would owe for a week at the inn.

"Thanks a lot," said George, taking the bills. "Cash flow . . . et cetera . . . Not that we're in trouble financially or anything."

"Too much information, George," Magdalene muttered through clenched teeth.

"I bought all this liquor for the Fiction People, you see, and now Professor Eggman says they don't even drink. Not any of them. I don't see the least thing literary about any of it—"

Magdalene snapped the money out of George's hand.

"That's right, darling," said George. "Why don't *you* take the money."

"If you're going into Tyburn," Tim asked Magdalene, "do you think I might catch a ride?"

Magdalene looked at her guest as if she suspected and fully appreciated—indeed, encouraged—ulterior motives. She raised her chin and tossed her hair. Then replaced her beret, in front of a mirror. George looked as if he were watching a train wreck.

"We can have lunch," Magdalene said flatly to Tim, though glancing at George. "I'll be outside."

The front door slammed. Tim looked at George. George looked pale.

"My wife is unhappy," said George. "She wants a divorce."

"I'm sorry," said Tim.

"I've often wondered why civilized sexual variety is impossible without tremendous loss of property."

"Because we're provincials."

"Exactly."

"Well, sorry, George."

"Not your fault," said George, puttering with the buffet. "Italy, for instance, percolates with adultery. If I lived in Italy, I could have sex with a woman who really liked me, and then I could come home to something like this."

"I'll talk to her if you like."

"She's confused," George said.

"Ah."

Tim had lived long enough to know that whenever people said they were confused, they weren't confused at all, but contemplating betrayal with awesome clarity. If Tim had gotten a chance, he would have said this—which was one of the problems with Tim. For an insipid hero in a particular narrative tradition, he was very considerably proactive. However, Magdalene was already in the car, blowing the horn dementedly.

"I suppose I ought to object to you two going off together," said George, brightening, and rubbing his hands together, "but in my opinion, in this world you usually get what you're afraid of. Therefore I remain serene."

"That's good policy, George."

"Au revoir," said George.

"Yes," said Tim, and grabbing his coat and duffel, he went after Magdalene.

Chapter 10

A Chapter in Which a Great Deal
Is Explained, Really

Professor Eggman, as has been stated, had also gone out that morning. What has not been made clear is that he went into town, via Tyburn Taxi, to collect Mr. Glowery. In the midst of the calls from the canceling workshoppers, Mr. Glowery had phoned to report that he was being held prisoner by *John Wong*, and requested that Professor Eggman pick him up at a donut shop in the center of Tyburn. Professor Eggman arrived early, marched into the donut shop, and announced unaccountably, "I am here for Mr. Negro."

Something was going wrong with the literary part of Professor Eggman's mind, and it filled him with fear and dubiety. Lately words had gone batty on him: driving into Tyburn, he had read a sign that read "Hardware for Sale" as "Hardcore the Clown." Some connector had shorted out, and transformed his ordinary world of signs and semantics into what appeared to be postmodern gibberish. Professor Eggman was struggling gamely to remain afloat in his own artistic reality, even as he was overswarmed by protean logos and clearly heretical insights.

Professor Eggman had actually written that morning, on one of his slips of paper, while still partially in a dream state: *I am what I say I am: I am the Negro Bakerman*, and had parsed it thus: *I am not a baker or a Negro and there is no such thing as a Negro and if there were I would say something else anyway, so there fore* [sic] *I am what I say I am which is the Negro Bakerman.* The tone of vehement authority is indispensable, the Professor had thought later, while shaving, when one is saying something (1) inaccurate and (2) meaningless. Professor Eggman had been filled all morning with the not easily dismissed conviction that one could write "Negro" because it meant absolutely nothing and neither did anything else.

Unbeknownst to himself, Professor Eggman was flickering at the edge of literary relevancy. Now he stood blinking in the doorway of a provincial donut shop, betrayed by words for the ten-thousandth time in two weird days of what appeared to be General Paralysis of the Insane—having just shouted the unspeakable word "Negro" at an audience consisting (thank God!) of two crippled Sicilian fishermen, a Caucasian vagrant, a Transcarpathian biker prostitute in a rabbit-fur coat, and an exhausted Iranian servitor.

Professor Eggman, in his glen plaid scarf, was tall, fat, and sixty, with weak darting blue eyes and a somewhat off-kilter face frozen in a mask of pedagogical dignity beneath a pillarlike Russian hat. Dressed in blue work clothes he would have looked like a degenerate. In his rich tweeds, however, he had an uneasy majesty. He collected himself (the true Professor Eggman assembled like a storm), consulted his watch grimly, and decided that he had just enough time to have a cup of coffee in peace before the dubious Mr. Glowery either made his appointment or didn't.

Coffee was a very serious matter. Professor Eggman

was very serious about everything, in fact, especially the things he undertook to ingest. He was the sort of man who liked attributives with his comestibles and potables. It gave Professor Eggman great pleasure to understand that he was consuming coffee from a *Jamaica* bean, or *Hadley* asparagus. Words had specific, sacred freight (moral, social, political, etc.—all of which used to be understood simply as *religious*), which is why it was terrifying when you—that is, Professor Eggman—looked at a book and it said "Prose and Worse" instead of the "Prose and Verse" you had every reason to expect. If words were for play and even "Negro" meant nothing, really, Professor Eggman was all fucking done.

Words were very serious indeed. Recently, on a visit to the University of Iowa, he had been offered an inferior (i.e., nameless) burgundy. He had smiled thinly and replaced the glass on a tray, as if it had contained an excrement. Had there been a swanky descriptor attached to the wine, though, he would have drunk it as if his duodenum had been full of napalm.

A man came in and cut in front of Professor Eggman, who listened with his infallible novelist's ear (his wife, at any rate, said that his ear was infallible) to a grammatically appalling conversation of the sort that found its way into Professor Eggman's moralistic fiction (which was ordinarily about simple working-class people who knew far less about themselves than one would reasonably expect, and always, *always*, encountered an academic who managed to show them a Way Forward). Professor Eggman had an almost medieval and intensely material chain-of-being view of the social order, and believed (as he had to, really) that it was *education* that put you at the top of that chain, as an aristocrat (which Professor Eggman was, as you could tell by his hat).

"Yeah gimme a regular and one a them donits with the colored jimmies there."

The orderer then actually licked his thumb before peeling a bill off his wad and paying. He went off audibly slurping coffee.

It was Professor Eggman's turn. The exhausted Iranian was staring at him with fifth-shift immigrant exhaustion.

"I don't suppose," said Professor Eggman with an uneasy jocularity, "that it would do me any good to ask what *sort* of coffee you have."

"We have coffee."

"No sort of . . ." Professor Eggman searched for the word.

"We have coffee."

"Right-o," said the Professor, unpleasantly. "I'll have a 'coffee.'"

"Rigola?" demanded the Iranian.

"Pardon?"

"Rigola?"

"Oh yes, yes, yes, regular coffee, sir, for regular fellows."

"Faggot," said one of the crippled fishermen, under his breath.

"What size recolor?"

"Oh, I don't know. Heavens. Large? And a plain 'donit.'"

Professor Eggman paid for his purchases, and carried them to a table at an aquariumlike corner of the shop, where he saw that his napkin, instead of "Donut Den," read "Fuck Off." He used it to mop up the table anyway—at least it was good for that. He uncapped his coffee and took a sip which nearly burned his face off, and spilled coffee over the table. "Outrageous," Professor Eggman tried to say, but unfortunately it came out—the worst thing yet—as:

"This is art, you cunts."

Everyone stared at Professor Eggman, who now had nothing to say for himself whatsoever, and therefore harrumphed, dug into his briefcase, and began to magisterially inscribe to Mr. Glowery or Negro or whoever he was a copy of *The Best Short Stories in the History of the World.* He signed it with a flourish and before he could stop himself dated it 1599. He stared at the page with a wild surmise. It read: "To Mr. Negro this mirrour." Outside the steamed windows, snow began to flurry in the air.

"This is art, you cunt, anyway," said Professor Eggman affably, to the elderly priest who had just sat down at the next table.

Chapter 11

Adultery and Oranges

The Hawthornes' car was, predictably, a Volvo. Tim cleared the snow off the windows, shivering in the wind, then got in with Magdalene. She was not a large woman and looked particularly small behind the wheel. She drove very badly indeed, clashing the gears and invariably shifting at the wrong moment, yet all the time looking completely arch. The Volvo stalled twice on the snowy (and tide-imperiled) causeway that led from the inn to the coast road, but then pottered along nicely. Driving into town, Tim and Magdalene did not speak. Tim was intensely conscious of Magdalene. She was very likely out of her mind, but he had never found that unattractive in women. His ideal, in fact, was the romantic, olive-skinned shrew who one instant was flinging a plate at one's head and the next was in tears like a Renaissance Madonna. Magdalene was both dark and unstable. She had a lush and sultry mouth. She definitely qualified.

Tim considered the situation. He was young, but had made some several observations about sex. He had a spot-on theory about infidelity: that a person who would cheat on another person, with you, would invariably cheat on you, with someone else. Then again, you really weren't required to be around when it was time for the person to cheat on you. This is practiced less than you think it would be, thought Tim.

In Tyburn, Magdalene just barely managed to parallel park her car, and she and Tim went into the bank. Magdalene in her beret, waiting in line for a teller, watched Tim disappear into the manager's office. She could see the two men through the glass partition. The manager was a perfect bastard, in Magdalene's experience. Yet here was the holder of the Hawthornes' as yet unpaid—and frankly, unpayable—third mortgage being unusually cordial to Tim, a complete stranger. Magdalene watched in amazement as the manager whisked out to get Tim a cup of coffee. She was personally affronted. She elevated her chin.

"Aren't you the lady out the inn?" asked a workie brute who stood behind Magdalene in line. The man was slurping coffee from a Drunken Grownups cup.

"I seriously doubt it," said Magdalene.

"Your husband owes me a thousand bucks."

Lacerated, Magdalene struck back. "For what? Elocution lessons?"

"I'm Jimmy Novella. I sold him the silk-screen setup for his bumpa stickers. He paid me half and said that I'd get the rest last week."

It was true: the apparatus was hidden in one of the sheds.

"My husband does not make bumper stickers, Mr. Novella," said Magdalene.

"Not if I find him," said Mr. Novella.

Magdalene transacted her business, and then waited for Tim on the sidewalk, holding her beret on her head. The wind was kicking up brilliantly. Tim emerged from the bank and with some difficulty lit a cigarette.

"I don't like to wait," said Magdalene.

"I'm sorry."

She visibly sulked. Tim was charmed. The woman had no manners. Like most subtle people, Tim secretly liked that. It's why the English plague the Mediterranean, downing retsina in low tavernas, soaking up the flowers of crudity.

"Are you rich?" demanded Magdalene.

"Yes," said Tim.

"What did you do in the bank? You were in there an awfully long time."

"I got some traveler's checks," said Tim, "and rented a safe-deposit box."

"What did you put in the safe-deposit box?"

"Manuscripts," Tim said.

They headed off down the street, walking through a light snow. Magdalene was not encouraged by the mention of manuscripts. George had manuscripts. In Magdalene's experience, manuscripts were things that received a great deal of attention, were committed to the mail with infinite hope and absurd momentousness, and were invariably returned without comment, occasioning in George a three-to-four-month drinking binge. She had never heard of manuscripts being put in safe deposit, though, and the idea absorbed her. It was at least remotely conceivable that some manuscripts were valuable, though not George's. This was not completely fair to George. He had once produced a novel in two weeks, put it (an eminently publishable bildungsroman, filled with künstlerschuld well handled) into the mailbox, but then panicked. After failing to crowbar the rural mailbox open, he had run it over with his car. George retrieved his only masterpiece from a whirlwind of postcards, and burned it in a leaf basket in Vermont. So much for George.

Tim had an eye out for clothing stores. He liked the town of Tyburn instantly. It was somewhat decayed. In some of the shops there were signs in Italian, and signs in English reading "We Speak Italian" (which surely should have been in Italian). In the cold air, there was a strangely attractive stink of fish and diesel fuel. From somewhere came a cascade of carillon bells, which sounded pleasant, if out of tune. Across the street a crowd was gathered around a man who had fallen off a ladder while taking down municipal Christmas lights. Magdalene was pleased to identify Jimmy Novella.

"I hate my husband," said Magdalene as they walked.

"I can see that, Mrs. Hawthorne."

"We have an open marriage, though," said Magdalene.

"Ah."

Tim sensed accurately that this was a new development, which had something to do with him, and instead of responding, suggested that they go into a clothing store. Magdalene did not mind: she was delighted. She took absolute charge, tearing things roughly out of Tim's hands if they did not agree with her sensibilities, examining him shrewdly when he emerged from the dressing room. She was unbelievably rude to the salesclerk, a sad-eyed man with a nasty hangover who as it happened had spent the night drinking cordials with Mr. Glowery. He had picked up Mr. Glowery hitchhiking in a distrait and susceptible condition. After staying up until six a.m. listening to Mr. Glowery talk about *John Wong*, he hadn't even scored. He flinched every time Magdalene spoke.

The store was a bit provincial—the highest order of human being it had outfitted was a lobsterman elected to the city council—but Tim found one good dark suit that needed no alterations, and he bought some shirts, the least horrible tie available, a pair of shoes, a suitcase, and some socks and underwear. He had decided to wear suits from now on, a severe eccentricity for a painter. He'd also decided that he would spend a week or two in London, buying very, very good clothes and large, anachronistic traveling trunks, before heading on to pick up his paintings in Como and proceeding to Venice by train to rent a palazzo. A small one, probably: Tim had no idea what they cost these days.

They went to lunch in a seafood house, Tim in his new dark suit and Magdalene in her beret. Magdalene opened a compact and fixed her lipstick at the table. She was going for a noir effect but the restaurant lent itself more to light comedy. Tim sat smiling indulgently as the waitress, who wore a name tag, and whose name was Nutmeg, executed a travesty of wine service and wrestled faultily and finally almost fatally with the cork.

Two tables over, César Pilosi, private detective, boorishly forked meat out of the tail of a lobster, and ate it deliriously, as he had not seen food or a bed for forty-eight hours. He had not dared to sleep in his rented car—you didn't sleep in your car when you worked for Jesus Castro—and he was beginning to hallucinate. Still, he was on the job, and he scribbled in his notebook: "1:37 p.m. Subject appears to be getting laid." When Magdalene took off her jacket, he noted professionally: "Nice tits."

They certainly were. Both Tim and Mr. Pilosi stopped chewing their food.

Chapter 12

The One-Legged Seafaring Man

At the inn there was suddenly another guest, of all things, and this guest was much less to George's taste than Tim Picasso. Jesus Castro arrived alone in a white Mercedes with a rental sticker, carrying a large alligator suitcase, and looking, in a huge-shouldered alpaca over-coat, to be intensely upset at the environment. He looked up at the New England winter sky with a degree of personal enmity. George took his bag and held the door as they entered the Admiral Benbow, and then raced around behind the desk. George had less experience of Latinos than Jesus Castro had with the Massachusetts winter. But he was liberal, and consequently nicer to Mr. Castro than he would have been to anyone who was not Latino, unless of course they were African-American.

Jesus Castro, who was rude to everybody, regarded George as if he were from another planet.

"You give me room."

"Smoking or nonsmoking?" asked George compassionately.

"Whatever. I smoke if I want."

"Of course! And how long will you be with us?"

"What?"

"How long will you be our guest?"

"Two tree days. Not your business."

Laboriously, an unlit cigar in his mouth, Jesus Castro

signed the registration ledger. George reversed it delicately.

"Thank you, Mr. . . . Wassermann."

"You got problem sometime with my name?"

"No. No, of course not."

Jesus Castro ignited a cigar. "I need two room more tonight, guy named Pilosi."

"Pilosi," repeated George idiotically.

"Another guy come later, too, fly up from Miami."

George had been savagely disappointed that the Fiction People, with the exception of their maître, the problematical Eggman, were staying elsewhere. But now, what with Professor Eggman, Tim Picasso, Messrs. Wassermann and Pilosi, the unnamed late arrival, and of course Mr. Briscoe (Mr. Briscoe might have been dead at the lighthouse, but he had paid months in advance), that meant *six rooms rented*. The hotel was suddenly fully booked in the middle of February. Visions of solvency danced in George's head.

"Oh I understand perfectly," said George, which was what he always said when he had no idea whatsoever what was going on.

"You got phone?" asked Jesus Castro.

In the lobby there was an object that was George's pride and joy, an actual English telephone box of the old style, painted bright red. Jesus Castro went and worked the door.

"Where you get this?"

"In England," George said, reverently. George was an Anglophile of the foaming variety.

"Nice. How much you sell these to me?"

"It's not for sale, actually."

"How much?"

After selling the phone box to Mr. Wassermann (although George was dimly certain that he could not really be named Wassermann), George took his new guest upstairs and showed him to Norman's Woe, which had an unfortunate name ("Who's Norman?" people would ask), but which was in fact one of the most comfortable rooms at the Admiral Benbow. Jesus Castro stood in the doorway, staring at the narrow bed; the dresser with mismatched knobs; the writing table and Sheraton chair jammed into a wallpapered dormer. A framed needlepoint was on the wall:

The skipper he stood beside the helm,
His pipe was in his mouth,
And he watched how the veering flaw did blow
The smoke now West, now South.

"You go to be shit me," said Jesus Castro.

"I beg your pardon?"

"Show me room."

"This is the room, I'm afraid. I'm awfully sorry."

"These is all you got? You tell me these is all you got some time for me today?"

"I'm afraid it is. Look, Mr. Wassermann, obviously you're a man with a taste for the better things in life—"

Jesus Castro acknowledged this inarticulately.

"—and I'm afraid we don't have any of those things here. This is a bed-and-breakfast."

"I don' want no fucking breakfast."

"Well, there is a better room, with a fireplace, but I'm

afraid that there's another guest installed at the moment. He might be persuaded to exchange with you. I could ask."

"Who these guest?" asked Jesus Castro, as if he really had no idea.

"A young man."

"Never mine I take these one room today. Room phone."

"I'm afraid that none of our rooms have telephones."

"You go to be shit me," said Jesus Castro.

"In point of fact, Mr. Wassermann, I'm not."

"Okay. Leave." Mr. Castro peeled off a fifty from a tremendous roll of bills, and slapped the banknote into George's belatedly extended hand.

"You treat me good, I treat you good." Jesus Castro smiled. "That is the rule of life. Don' forget him like some guy did maybe. Right now, I take nap." He puffed his cigar with extraordinary force. "Where to get girl?"

"I beg your pardon?" asked George.

"Get me girl. I go to relax."

"You don't mean a prostitute, do you?"

"I go to relax."

"Well. We don't have much call. Are you sure you mean a prostitute?"

Mr. Castro stared at him.

"I'll see what I can do," said George.

Chapter 13

In Which Steam Rises and Snow Falls

Tim and Magdalene went to a hot-tub establishment run on ersatz Japanese principles by local chai-drinking dirt wizards. Magdalene had suggested that Tim come along to her hot-tub appointment since her friend had unexpectedly canceled. Actually, Magdalene had telephoned Portia Waxwood from the restaurant and told her to fuck off. It wasn't the sort of hot-tub place where you got robes. Magdalene disrobed with calm valor in the snow and cold air, hanging her beret and then the rest of her things on a peg, while Tim nervously feigned interest in various features of the tub platform, which was on the roof of an old building by the harbor. Finally he took a deep breath, removed his clothes, and clambered into the tub with affected unconcern. They sat quietly on opposite sides of the wooden tub. The agitation of the water concealed their bodies. The snow began to fall harder: where before it had flurried in the storm twilight, now it obviously meant business, as if it thought it was falling all over Ireland.

"I'm actually a dancer," said Magdalene.

"Hmm."

"At least I was."

Magdalene neglected to mention that she had also failed superbly as an actress. She looked at Tim nervously.

"I'm much older than you," said Magdalene. "How old *are* you?"

"Twenty-two."

"Well. It's not as if we came here in a romantic situation. We didn't come here to—do anything."

"Oh, obviously," said Tim.

"You do understand why we came."

"Yes, your bad back hurts, and you need two people, and your friend couldn't make it." Tim was suddenly less nervous than Magdalene.

"Exactly."

There was another snowy silence. Tim remembered a *National Geographic* cover with snow monkeys immersed in a hot spring in wintry Japan.

"My back is feeling better," Magdalene announced.

"Oh good," said Tim insincerely.

"This is nice."

"Yes, it is. I suppose."

Magdalene gave Tim a curious look. Tim was as sybaritic as the next guy, but he was also Irish Catholic (the O'Picassoins are an old and noble clan), which meant that he had to wryly belittle all sybaritic experiences, in the course of fully enjoying them.

"You have to come here with someone, you see. They won't let you come alone. I mean, you can pass out and drown, or boil to death." She giggled. "This is the first time I've been here after I've been drinking."

"I wish it was in a pill," said Tim, who had downed two bottles of wine personally.

"I feel like the top of my head is coming off."

Magdalene stretched and her foot brushed Tim's. He froze, excruciated, biting his lips.

"Isn't it funny," said Magdalene, a little too loudly,

"how in our culture we immediately associate nudity with sex. We don't bathe together, for instance. In Japan they bathe with each other, and it isn't erotic at all."

That was it: Tim lit a cigarette.

"Have you ever been to Japan?" asked Tim, snapping his Zippo shut.

"No," said Magdalene.

"Then don't tell me what happens in the bathtubs."

"Do you find me attractive?" Magdalene demanded.

This is always an odd question. Men find almost everyone attractive. Even if Tim had found Magdalene far less attractive than she was (and believe me, she was profoundly attractive), his body (alpha, male, etc.) would have wanted to pump her full of zygotic material before someone else did—and then go find someone else to whom to do the same thing.

"Yes, obviously I find you attractive," said Tim. "But we do have free will. Liberum arbitrium."

"I always wanted to learn French," said Magdalene. "It's so civilized."

"That's what Augustine was on about. It's not like I'm . . . biology's . . . puppet. Or fiend."

"In different circumstances," said Magdalene, emboldened, arching her back and setting her olive breasts afloat, "this would be erotic."

"Different circumstances," Tim repeated dully, looking up at the snow.

"I mean, if we were attracted to each other."

"I just established that I *was* attracted to you and had *chosen* not to act on it, in an act of, er, Augustinian free will.

Were I less morally alert—or apprehensive about being killed by your husband—I would have already lunged across the pool at the first indication of probable consent."

Magdalene without warning levered herself out of the tub and sat on the redwood deck in the falling snow, her back against the board screen that shielded the roof-tub from the view of fishermen in the harbor. She loosened her hair. Steam rose. Snow fell. She didn't *look* like someone who thought Latin was French.

"Don't you want to get out for a minute? It feels good."

"No, no, no," said Tim. "I'm fine."

Magdalene slipped back into the water. One of her feet touched Tim's. Tim opened his mouth to say something trivial, but then launched himself across the tub instead. A good third of the water flooded noisily out of the tub while they copulated like something out of a nature film. The situation became impossible: Tim lifted Magdalene onto the snow on the redwood deck. It was an interesting complex of sensations. Magdalene with a stifled shriek had her first penetration orgasm in ten years—or since marriage. (It wasn't George's fault, of course: he'd never thought of snow and boiling water.) Tim haggardly stared down at Magdalene. The snowfall had turned into a full-on blizzard.

"Oh thank God," said Magdalene.

It was at this point that the door was suddenly opened. The hot-tub attendant appeared through the steam, carrying a portable telephone.

"What the fuck do you think you're doing," said Tim.

"Telephone for Mrs. Hawthorne."

Magdalene (who had had another rattling orgasm from the oddly pleasant shock of being surprised in flagrante by a stranger), took a brief personal moment and then snapped her fingers and took the phone.

"Perhaps you could leave us alone now?" said Tim.

"Certainly, sir. Please have the courtesy to think of the next patron and avoid you-know-what in the tub."

"I'm not *in* the tub! Now get out."

"Enjoy your tubbing."

"It's not a verb."

"Yes, George?" said Magdalene, uncovering the mouth-piece.

Tim tried respectfully to disengage himself but Magdalene had locked her ankles behind his bum.

"Well, look in the phone book under 'Escorts,' George. What do you think those are?"

Tim's eyes widened.

"No, I didn't drop him off, George, Portia Waxwood canceled, so he's here with me." Tim heard George shouting.

"Oh George, don't be an asshole," said Magdalene. "I'm here for my back, and we're both in our underwear."

She switched off the phone abruptly, and she and Tim slid back into the tub.

Chapter 14

The Strange Deliverance of Mr. Glowery

On the sidewalk outside the donut shop, Professor Egg-man observed deliriously that the snow had begun to fall almost laterally from the black north. It was not a Currier and Ives situation: it was a whacking, brutal, nor'east blizzard. The Professor was forced to wait outside for his taxi, for he had made himself persona non grata in the "donit" shop—he couldn't even stand in *front* of the donut shop, after all the involuntary shouting of "Negro" and "cunt" he had been doing—so there he was, whitening with snow in front of a neighboring video store, under a sign that read: "You Want the Movies? We Got the Movies. You Do the Math." A cutout of Michael Caine in *Get Carter*, toppled by the wind, leaned against Professor Eggman lasciviously, then spun away into the whitening road.

Professor Eggman grappled his collar shut with one hand, and stood there, bent against the gale, holding his unnecessary briefcase in the other. Through the blinding snow he slowly made out an emaciated figure of a pirate, which stared at him from the doorway of a restaurant called Cap'n Stumpy's. Professor Eggman wandered closer. The pirate had an eyepatch and a parrot and a handful of leaflets. The Professor was at first convinced that the pirate was a *statue* of some sort, but then he noticed (with difficulty through the intensifying blast) that the pirate was motile. Also, he was holding like a breviary a copy of Mr. Glowery's novel about growing up like Mr. Glowery.

"Pardon me," said Professor Eggman, "but where did you obtain that novel?"

"I wrote it," said Mr. Glowery hollowly, less to Professor Eggman than the elements.

"Mr. Glowery is a very interesting young novelist," said the Professor. "He is not a restaurant pirate."

"I have to pay for my drinks," said Mr. Glowery, crying.

Archy Lafata, in his chef's toque, pushed open the door of Cap'n Stumpy's.

"Hand out them leaflets like I told you," he said to Mr. Glowery. "Or I'll pop you so hard you'll wish I *was* the Society in the Tower."

"Is this man a novelist?" demanded Professor Eggman.

"What do I look like, posterity?" asked Archy Lafata.

Mr. Glowery, still crying, reflected that Mr. Lafata looked very much like Posterity indeed.

"Good God!" roared Professor Eggman. "Mr. Glowery?"

Mr. Glowery nodded sadly. Snot coming from his nose had formed into an impressive icicle.

"This guy's into me for drinks," said Archy. "I got him cocked and he tries the old bank machine trick. Oh right, he's gonna pay me later."

"This is indecent!"

"Hey," said Archy shiftily. "I didn't touch the guy and neither did my partner."

Professor Eggman produced his billfold. "How much does he owe you for drinks?"

"A thousand dollars."

"Ridiculous," said Professor Eggman. "How could any-one have a thousand dollars' worth of drinks?"

"You give me a grand or that guy's my pirate until next month."

"I'll telephone the police," said Professor Eggman with a singular lack of menace.

Archy Lafata instantly punched Professor Eggman in the head. It was not a very good punch, and Professor Eggman's Russian hat absorbed most of the blow, but the Professor was not used to being struck, and he instantly fell down upon the sidewalk. Archy's partner (who had in fact touched Mr. Glowery, rather a lot) appeared in the doorway and wrestled Archy back into the restaurant. Simultaneously a taxi arrived, and Mr. Glowery, dressed as a pirate, got into it. Professor Eggman crawled through the snow in a panic and scrambled in after him.

"Good God in heaven," said Professor Eggman. "I was just assaulted."

"*I* have moral syphilis," said Mr. Glowery.

Nothing to Write Home About

"Thank God you're here," said George. "I don't know what to do. There's an awful man in Norman's Woe who wants a prostitute, as I told you on the phone, and old Mr. Whistler and his nurse arrived and want tea. It's turning into a nor'easter, and we don't have any fucking cucumbers."

"Improvise," said Magdalene, and went upstairs.

"We have a sort of bullshit afternoon tea," explained George to Tim. "Or we do when there are customers, which there aren't usually. We used to have an old woman that did it, but she wanted money or something. We had to 'let her go,' I believe is the locution. Actually she's suing us. Tell me, Mr. Picasso, did you have sex with my wife?"

"Yes, I did," said Tim. "I'm sorry."

"I see." George looked as if he did. "Christ."

"It just happened."

"Well, that's that. Do you know anything about prostitutes?"

"No."

"So, I've been calling escort services all over Boston, and none of them will say if they're prostitution rings."

"I imagine not."

"Look, I promised Mr. Wassermann a dominatrix open to the idea of straight sex in case he feels he has to prove anything. Nothing with an attitude, in other words. Do you think you could call around and make inquiries? Frankly I'm in a jam."

"I'll see what I can do."

"God bless you," said George. He shouted to a deaf old man in the parlor (that is, Mr. Whistler, who did not hear him) that tea would be ready presently, and grabbed his coat and ran out the front door. He ran back in a moment later, with snow in his eyebrows. "She's got to be blond, and she's got to have bondage paraphernalia. Whips, hoods, whatnot. Mr. Wassermann wants her for two days, and he's paying five thousand dollars cash."

"Who is Mr. Wassermann?" asked Tim.

George plunged out into the blizzard again without answering. A moment later Tim heard the Volvo roar away toward town. He went behind the desk and looked at the open Yellow Pages. There were a number of escort services listed. He called the first one whose ad featured a photograph of a woman in leather, gave his name as Hawthorne, and with some tact negotiated precisely what the invisible—and unimaginable—Mr. Wassermann required. Then he went upstairs, locked his door, put the back of a chair under the doorknob just in case George became unreasonable (though if George wanted to be unreasonable he'd undoubtedly enter through the closet shared with the Easterly Room), got into bed, and fell immediately asleep.

In the room on the other side of the Easterly (which mercifully didn't share a closet), Jesus Castro was slowly loading the ammunition clip of a machine pistol with explosive cartridges. He had turned up the heat in the room as far as it would go, and was finally comfortable enough to sit around in his yellow bikini underwear, which was itself an essential component of his relaxation style. Jesus Castro was well insulated to begin with: he had more hair on his back and shoulders than seven ordinary men had on their heads. While he loaded the clip, he chewed on his half-smoked cigar. The room was blue with acrid smoke.

Despite what the Israeli machine pistol suggested, Jesus Castro was not an unreasonable man. He had expected the money to be stolen—he *always* expected his money to be stolen—he would have certainly stolen it himself—and he had a high regard for people who thought as he did. He was a businessman, true, and business was business. But he was also a human being, as he kept reminding people before he hurt, killed, or mutilated them. He thought of himself, furthermore, as a compassionate student of human nature. He had no intention, at present, of killing Tim Picasso if the money was returned. He relished the idea, in fact, of having a few drinks with him, a few laughs, and then, after explaining the exigencies of business, blowing off Tim's kneecaps with a burst of automatic-weapons fire. Tim would be left alive enough to regret having fucked with Jesus Castro. Jesus Castro always did this with people: he thought it was clever; but it wasn't all that clever. Jesus Castro was himself the subject of thirty-seven official hit contracts and upward of fifty in-progress Senecan revengings. It was better to kill people.

There was a sharp knock at the door, and Mr. Castro looked around. Hastily he closed his suitcase, which contained more weapons, including some grenades he wanted to try out if he got the opportunity. He arranged himself on the edge of the bed, with the machine pistol cocked on his lap, concealed by a silk dressing gown which was covered with Chinese characters. He took the cigar from his mouth.

"Come Ing," said Jesus Castro.

The door was opened by a dark woman, unknown to Mr. Castro. She batted theatrically at the smoke. Mr. Castro examined her shrewdly and decided that she was not a prostitute.

"Are you smoking a cigar?" asked Magdalene.

"Who the fuck are you?" asked Jesus Castro, politely.

"No cigars are to be smoked in the rooms. It's stinking up the hallway."

"Fuck you," said Mr. Castro. "Get out."

Magdalene opened her mouth to speak, but then noticed that Mr. Wassermann appeared to be naked. One hand was beneath the Chinese robe that was draped over his lap, and the robe was distended by what Magdalene could only assume was a bong, or an enormous erection. Still, she held her ground.

"I'm allergic to smoke."

This was not quite true. Magdalene, like many "smoke-allergic" people, was allergic to smoke only when it was being produced by people she had no interest in cultivating socially.

"Chinga tu madre. Get the fuck out."

Magdalene stepped forward with the unholy light of battle in her eye.

"No, Mr. Wassermann. *You'll* get the fuck out if you don't put that *cigar* out, and if you don't like it, you can talk to the police about it when they throw you off the porch."

Jesus Castro sat openmouthed for a moment.

"Hey, wait a ming, I put him out, okay?"

Jesus Castro did so, chuckling pleasantly as he rapidly stubbed the cigar into a pink conch shell, or skillen, causing the low fusion of three thousand—and then less than a hundred—years of sexual symbolism. At any rate, Jesus Castro liked women with an attitude, and he was rather disappointed that Magdalene hadn't come to torture him.

"Thank you."

"No police."

"I don't know what you're doing under that robe, but stop it," said Magdalene, gravely, and closed the door.

She went along the hallway to her room, showered, dressed, and after a fond look and an inconclusive tapping at Tim's door, frowned and went downstairs to deal with George.

Despite the fierce exchange with Mr. Wassermann, Magdalene was in a terrifically good mood—radiant with adultery—and she even chatted with—or shouted hospitably at—the deaf Mr. Whistler, an invalid (as Anglophile as her embarrassing husband, if not more so), who had for some time not been able to make high tea at the Admiral Benbow, because of some sort of incontinence. It was unfair on Magdalene's part, however, to think of Mr. Whistler as an Anglophile: he wasn't. He was merely a codfish Bostonian who was raised eating high tea and using Edwardian sporting slang and had no other idea how to behave. At any rate, Mr. Whistler was well past imitating anyone now. Chortling deafly, he appeared to be in a very good mood. His nurse, Lucille, sulked in an armchair with a look of belligerent impatience as Mr. Whistler sat waiting, neither belligerent nor impatient, nor definitively conscious, for tea. In the kitchen, George, returned from the store, and still in his snowy coat, was feverishly arranging cucumber sandwiches on a silver tray. Real silver, too. (George didn't know this, or he would have sold it with the rest of the silver.)

"*Tea*," George said. "Wilde could have killed this habit with a one-liner. Pervert."

"I'm divorcing you, George," Magdalene announced, coming breezily into the kitchen.

"Excellent!" shouted George.

"I'm *divorcing* you," Magdalene repeated.

George didn't seem to care.

"Splendid. You have infinite choice in the realm of nature. Do something Sartrean and authentic. Join the circus, reduce Harfleur, have the Cobb salad. Run for president. I don't give a shit, and neither does anyone else, and neither would God. Look, will you make the tea, and hot the pot for God's sake, the old bastard will notice. It's all he notices."

Magdalene cut open tea bags and shook the loose leaves into the pot.

"You had sex with Mr. Picasso," George said.

"I did not!" Magdalene was indignant. "Don't be ridiculous."

"You *did*."

"George, the idea is absurd. We were in our underwear. I told you."

"He *said* that you did."

Magdalene froze.

"Well," she said after a moment, "he's lying." She continued lightly with the tea.

"Magdalene, I asked him, 'Did you have sex with my

wife?' and he said, 'Yes, I did, George, I'm sorry.' I don't know if you understand."

"I suppose if he *insists*," said Magdalene.

She tried to think of what to say next.

"I was confused," she said finally, and drifted out of the room.

George stood for a moment, staring out at the blinding snow, and then, with the expression of man on the verge of hysterical collapse, carried the tray of sandwiches and tea lightly into the "conservatory," which is what he called the sunporch, because he was George.

Chapter 16

Mr. Briscoe Up Against It

Out on the island, in the lightkeeper's cottage, Mr. Briscoe had run out of firewood and coal and kerosene. His generator had run out of gasoline, he was unable to fix his radio, and he finally had decided to risk the return to the mainland through the heavy seas. The decision was not particularly sound, and Mr. Briscoe knew it, but it was one of those afternoons when he really couldn't give a shit. Furthermore, he had finished *The Riddle of the Sands*, *Greenmantle*, *At the Sign of the Golden Anchor* (how Mr. Briscoe wept when the little Maid of Annisquam saved the schooner *Federalist* from the British torch), three different versions of the Holy Bible, and a large-print book of cross-word puzzles—and he was nearly out of whiskey.

Off and on throughout the day, he had been trying in various ways to signal that fruit at the inn to have the Coast Guard come and rescue him from the island (or at least air-drop him some heater fuel, tobacco, whiskey, and for that matter maybe some grub), but the only result had been that Mr. Briscoe had lit his overcoat on fire while waving a flaming blanket from the turret of the lighthouse. Then, worse, he had fallen off a sectional ladder and broken his left arm while attempting to spray-paint "SOS" in suitably large letters on the landward side of the tower. The light tower now read "SO," as if it were some sort of anti-Freudian argument.

Flares would have been handy, but Mr. Briscoe had no flares, because he'd be damned if he'd pay what they asked for them down the marine supply. So as it began to get dark, Mr. Briscoe very clearly had only one option. He struggled one-armed into a red survival suit which was much too large for him. Then, after replacing his arm in his make-shift sling, which he'd constructed out of his own Sears briefs, he put his insulated cap on his head, pulled the earflaps down, and deliberately fastened the snap under his chin. He knelt briefly in prayer. When he opened the door of the cottage, it immediately blew off its hinges in a spray of splinters, hardware, and dislodged masonry, and cartwheeled off into the sea. "Blowing like friggin' Jesus," observed Mr. Briscoe, more laconically than most people would.

He had second thoughts about essaying the voyage ashore in his landing craft (which he had made, and not well, out of scrap metal), but now of course the lightkeeper's cottage had no door, and it already had shipped a good deal of green water and was missing several eastward windows. As for his other options, Mr. Briscoe didn't fancy his chances in the plywood dynamite shed or for that matter in the light tower itself, which had been blown apart and rebuilt in 1802, 1888, 1938, and 1960, and furthermore didn't have a door, either, because Mr. Briscoe hadn't made the new one yet. It was obvious to Mr. Briscoe that he was up against it whether he stayed or went. He took a last pull of Wild Turkey, tossed the bottle into the dead fireplace, and head down, staggered out of the cottage into the gale. He skidded and slipped down the icy path to the jetty, past rocks on which he had painted various Yankee mottoes, or bracing Catoan monostichs such as "Save Money," "Trust in the Lord," "Speak Your Mind," "Never Hit a Lady," and "Treat People Square and They Will Treat You White," as well as . . . well, a few more surreal yet still moralistic things he had painted on obscurer parts of the island. Mr. Briscoe had come to Art late in life, but it was his intention to leave the universe improved.

The swell was strong even in the leeward cove, and Mr. Briscoe's homemade landing craft, full of snow, was banging and gonging horribly against the granite jetty. Going down the icy ladder Mr. Briscoe managed to get one foot on the craft—retracted his foot—tried again—and then at a hazard let go of the ladder and jumped. As Mr. Briscoe went down, the vessel came up, and Mr. Briscoe, having severely miscalculated matters (and to be fair, he would have done no better sober), fell heavily into the steel barge. He cracked his head a good one and went out cold for a minute, but eventually he got manfully to his feet, shoveled some of the snow (not enough) out of the vessel, and decided (fatally) not to jettison its cargo of flagstone paving blocks. He started the diesel motor and cast off the lines. Blowing black smoke from its upright exhaust pipe, which Mr. Briscoe had made from ordinary plumbing stock he'd found at the dump, the landing craft reversed laboriously out of the cove. It cleared the jetty on the rise of a high swell, and then, coming about toward the headland, almost immediately foundered, swamped, and sank, leaving only Mr. Briscoe's toqued head floating above the slate-colored water. For a moment, above the sound of the storm, he thought he heard an ethereal chuckling.

He attempted to swim back to the island, but the tide carried him rapidly away from the jetty and toward the rocks of the mainland. He blew the CO_2 cartridge on his survival suit. As he was swept toward the shore by one fifty-foot sea after another, Mr. Briscoe spent some moments wishing he'd been nicer to people when he'd had the chance—he wished he'd had a chance to paint some more apothegms—he wished he'd put down the money for flares, no matter what they asked for them—and he also sincerely regretted that he'd never had a homosexual experience. He wasn't sure if he'd really *wanted* to have a homosexual experience, but he regretted not having had one to know if he had actually wanted one or not. If he had it to do all over again, he thought, he would have not have spent so much time over the Elks Club (where probationary sodomy was certainly not encouraged), and he would certainly have tried makeup. Why would you buy it over to Woolworth's, you damn fool, thought Mr. Briscoe, if you wasn't ever going to use it? Immensely philosophical, but occasionally screaming weakly, he was carried at increasing velocity toward shore, where the lights of the Admiral Benbow shone warmly in the violent caliginous darkness.

Some Incidents in the Tyburn Taxi

Yeah," said the cabdriver. "Quite a blow, they say."

"Who are 'they'?" inquired Professor Eggman exactingly. He was exhausted, and insane, but there was always enough of him left to be pedantic.

"I was being informal," said the driver.

"Is that what you call it?" said Professor Eggman.

The Tyburn Taxi, creeping through a rutted intersection, was nearly sideswiped by an enormous Department of Public Works plow with yellow emergency lights wheeling above its enormous cab, from which, Professor Eggman noticed, peered an incurious cretin wearing a hat identical to the fancy one worn by himself.

"Counter-jumper," roared Professor Eggman.

"That phrase has an interesting etymology," said the driver.

"What would you know about interesting entomologies?"

"*Etymologies,* ant-boy."

"Look," said Professor Eggman, "don't play the local cultured person, marooned amidst smocked, straw-chewing illiterates in some metaphysical Yorkshire, lying feverishly in wait with stockpiled philosophical disquisitions and trays of leprous fritillary rarities, for wayfarers conversible in Latinos."

"Conversant in Latinos?" asked the driver.

Professor Eggman was sitting openmouthed: he had intended to say none of this, and now he was responsible for it. Mr. Glowery pitched sideward and lay across his lap. Professor Eggman shoved him onto the floor, then realized that the man was a journalist who had come to interview him, and helped him back to his seat.

"Look here," said Professor Eggman. "I do not want to be driven anywhere, at any time, by a Victorian amateur of the arts. I want a normal, ignorant cabdriver." Professor Eggman removed his hat.

"It would be hubristic in me," said the driver, "to point out to you that you are shit out of luck on that one."

"I was just brutally assaulted by a baldheaded cook, who kidnapped this novelist and dressed him, unconvincingly, as a pirate. I have had all I want to do today, thank you, with the underclass." The Professor paused. "God help me. I said it."

"'Leprous fritillary rarities,'" said the driver.

"I'm sorry, I have a Nabokov," said Professor Eggman, who had intended to say "problem."

" . "

"I am late for my Fiction Workshop. I am in no mood to endure the worthless conversation of an autodidact. Thank you."

Another roaring plow, sparks flying from its street-scraping blade, came within an inch of striking the car. The taxi was lashed formidably with sand and salt. Mr. Glowery woke up briefly—clawed softly at the steamed window—and then with an expression of feeble rapture wrote *"John Wong"* in the moisture.

"Plows are out," said the driver laconically.

"For God's sake just get me to my hotel."

"Well, let's see. You're at the Admiral Benbow, sir, or the Samarra House?"

This was so lame and obvious a joke on the surface that Professor Eggman would have done well to look further into its mists and realize that he was being compared, in his social persona, to literature's John O'Hara, who, like so many unspeakable men before and after him, mistook Princeton, which is a college in New Jersey, for the gates of Elysian gentility.

"No," said Professor Eggman evilly. "And stop it with the literary references. Literary references! You have no idea who I am."

"Wait a minute, Commodore. Where *are* you staying?"

"As I told your employer when I telephoned from the 'donit' establishment—the Admiral Benbow."

"And you accuse me of literary references."

"What in God's name are you talking about?"

"Admiral Benbow."

Professor Eggman stared blankly.

"Them that dies is the lucky ones." The driver looked at him in the mirror. "Tip the black spot? If ever a sailor needed rum, Jim, it's me. Rum, Jim, I got the fidges!"

"What the Christ are you saying?"

"*Some* professor of English you are, sir."

"Oh, really. Who wrote . . ."

"You can't even think of one," jeered the driver.

"Rubbish. You do it. You test me. Tell me I'm not an English professor."

"Identify this passage . . ."

"Do your worst," said Professor Eggman.

"'Poor Ovid, that amorously writ in his youth the art of love, complained in his exile amongst the Getae of his wanton follies; and Socrates' age was virtuous though his prime was licentious. So, Gentlemen, my younger years had uncertain thoughts, but now my ripe days call on to repentant deeds, and I sorrow as much to see others wilful, as I delighted once to be wanton.'"

"It's Jacobean," said Professor Eggman uncertainly.

"Elizabethan."

"That's the same thing."

"No it isn't," said the driver. "At all. One cannot call an Elizabethan writer Jacobean, but one can call many Jacobean writers Elizabethan. Do you know why, sir?"

"It's a *riddle*," said Mr. Glowery, seraphic and drooling.

"We can call many Jacobean writers Elizabethan because they began in the fruitful reign of Elizabeth, even though they published after the succession of James."

"Shut up!"

"In fact, sir, you could call James's own pamphlets essentially Elizabethan, even though they were not only Jacobean, but written by James as well."

"Would you shut up. Do you have any idea who I am? I am . . . what I say I am. Not you."

"Academics invariably consider works by date of publication and fail to consider the fact that most writing, then, and now (like most homosexuals, come to think of it, however later they may *effloresce*), spends most of its time in a box in the closet."

"I told you to shut up!"

"By the time a book's in print, believe you me, Admiral, it's never dedicated to the woman it should be dedicated to. That's one of the great truths, of literature, sir. Probably the greatest, and the saddest. But you know, keep your dating systems, I'm not proposing a morphology of the amorphous. Then I'd be one of you."

Professor Eggman decided to ignore the man. He had a seminar for which to prepare. He dug in his briefcase, and snapped open his "teaching folder" to review his first lecture. Something very bad had happened to his notes, or his eyes, or his brain. The top page was still headed

LECTURE 1: THE SOCIAL RESPONSIBILITIES OF THE ARTIST

—but something hideous had happened to the text, which now read or seemed to read as follows:

May 21st. Mrs. Keble told me last evening the history of her cousin H, who last year found himself in some tropical place without a penny to his name. This young gentleman was forced to take passage on a *banana barge*, captained by an obscene and shiftless German. The banana-laden craft became becalmed at the Equator: the German died of fever. As the only other white man, Mrs. Keble's cousin found himself in de facto command of the vessel. At the first English port, he sold the cargo and vessel, paid off the crew, and then decamped for Lady Mortlake's. He was unaware that he was pursued by the actual owner of the boat, a Panamanian ruffian whose Christian name was indelicately that of Our Savior.

Jesus—I shall write the name—Castro subsequently arrived at Lady Mortlake's country house near Tring. Far from being ejected from the house, the ruffian endeared himself to all by demonstrating the use of a machete in opening coconuts (an art which had previously defeated the party), played bezique with the Duke of Clarence, seduced Lady Fanny ——, procured 5,000 pound from Lord J for a Colombian railroad scheme, cured Lavinia Rushmore's *Piles*, and converted a full one-third of the party to the Roman Catholic faith.

It was only after he was gone that the headless body of Mrs. K's cousin was discovered sitting upright in an armchair by the fire in the night nursery. It was also revealed that the unexpected guest (perhaps this is the title) had savagely violated old Mrs. Cotton, an invalid. The entire party was disappointed in "Jesus" (must change name) but were so charmed by him that they disposed of the headless body in the lake and opted not to call the police. The head was never found and it is supposed that "Jesus" (again, must change name) took it away with him. I feel that with a little effort and larger doses of opium I could develop this into a tale of 20,000 words, perhaps told in letters by a French *visiter*.

"Oh, my God in heaven," said Professor Eggman.

"I mean, let's look at *Hamlet*," said the driver, who was still talking.

Mr. Glowery vomited.

"It was first performed," said the cabdriver, "in the year of Elizabeth's death. Which was when, sir?"

"Ask me about magical realism or something."

"Don't take this personally, sir, but how much do you get paid?"

"More than *you*," said Professor Eggman.

The driver pulled instantly to the side of the road.

"Get out," he said.

Professor Eggman looked out the window. The cab was on a causeway in the middle of several miles of snow-blanketed marshland.

"Be reasonable," said Professor Eggman to the driver. He was nearly in tears. "How was I supposed to know you were not completely ignorant?"

"Even if I were, you shouldn't treat people like that. Get your shit—*and get out*."

"There's a blizzard. My friend . . . my . . ." Professor Eggman reconsidered. "My associate . . ." Professor Eggman looked at Mr. Glowery and considered again. "My companion is ill."

"*He* doesn't have to get out."

"We're not anywhere near the inn, you wretched auto-didact. Drive on!"

"What did you say?"

"I said, 'Drive on.'"

The cabdriver leaped out of the cab, came around to Professor Eggman's door, yanked it open in the instant before Professor Eggman could lock it, and dragged him out into the unplowed road. Then he got back into the Tyburn Taxi and drove away with Mr. Glowery. Professor Eggman got laboriously to his feet, a pathetic and solitary figure in the intensifying and Zhivagoan storm. Meanwhile Mr. Glowery, dressed as a Restoration mariner, was conveyed with all dispatch possible—which wasn't much—to the Admiral Benbow.

Chapter 18

Freud Was Wrong

O h dear," said George.

"Shut up, George," said Magdalene.

"You know I'm sexually insecure. What an awful thing to do. You did it on purpose, I know. It's a melodramatic appeal for attention."

"It's infidelity, George."

George stared at his hands in their dripping yellow rubber gloves. The sink was full of suds. Magdalene was sitting smugly at the kitchen table, eating cereal from a bowl.

"It's not an appeal for attention?"

"No. I don't want your attention."

George's face fell. "One always hopes, I suppose, for a kind of Freudian paradox. That is the chief appeal of Freud. It's very comforting to think that what is obviously happening isn't happening at all. Otherwise, life has a painful simplicity."

"I've already said that I want to leave you. I don't see what the problem is."

"What if we burned down the inn?" George asked suddenly.

"It's not insured."

"Would it look funny if we bought a lot of insurance and then burned it down?"

"*Fabulous* idea. Go ahead."

George picked up a glass of sherry and took a tremendous gulp.

"I'm not convinced," he said. "That would seem too obvious. It takes a great deal of sophistication to believe in chance. Freud said that. I don't know why. He didn't believe in it at all."

"I'm eating, George."

"We could buy insurance, burn the inn down, admit outright that it's a weird coincidence, and appeal to the worldliness of the fire marshal. Are you sure we can't just try therapy again?"

"I'm leaving you."

"I was so happy when we were doing therapy."

"You were on Halcion, George. You were smoking crack."

"Well, well," said George. He peeled off his yellow rubber gloves. "That's that, then, I suppose. Thanks for the marriage."

"No problem," said Magdalene.

Magdalene did, however, have a problem: she was penniless, and George didn't have any money she could get at, either. If Tim wasn't in love with her, she was in deep shit.

Mr. Whistler's nurse, Lucille, suddenly entered the kitchen. She was a large woman of African extraction, wearing a white uniform cap and big white shoes. There was a cardigan tied by its sleeves around her shoulders. Darkly, she said something neither George nor Magdalene could understand.

"I beg your pardon?" said George.

"Some trash bitch be in the lobby," said Lucille more distinctly.

"Ah. That will be for Mr. Wassermann. Thank you, Lucille."

"You keeps her away from Mr. Whistler. Old motherfucker will want to get hisself a throw. Finally I know what you runnin' here. Tea my ass."

George loped off down the hall, smoothing his hair back as usual, which now left his hair streaked with soapsuds. He tripped over an edge of the carpet in the passage. (By the time Lucille came into the kitchen, George had killed a full liter of Amontillado.) Once he'd recovered he banged into the wall, and knocked down a seascape, and then smashed his head on the corner of a table when he bent to pick it up. George was quite drunk. He staggered decorously into the lobby, where a small blond woman stood looking about superciliously. On the floor beside her was a cheap tartan bag, like an orphan's suitcase.

"Good afternoon," said George. "You must be the, ah . . ." He scurried behind the desk. "Thing. Mr. Wassermann is expecting you. Look, I don't know the drill with this sort of thing."

"You pay me and you do what I want."

"Oh." George stared at her. "I'm not going to pay you."

"What the fuck?"

"I mean, Mr. Wassermann's going to pay you. Do you really do things—with—implements, and so forth?"

"Sometimes."

"You have whips?" asked George interestedly.

"I have whips."

"What do you do with them?"

"What do you think I do with them?" She began to remove her black leather gloves.

"I see. You mean they have unacceptable thoughts, and so forth, and . . . and . . . everyone wears costumes and you . . . I see. It's all a bit Renaissance Faire for me, probably." George chuckled. "But maybe that's what it's all about. If you're going to be sexually humiliated you might as well do it intentionally. Oh, I'm being rude. Would you like a drink?"

"No."

"I'm only being hospitable. I am perfectly normal sexually. Whatever that is."

"I know your type, Wassermann. Cut the crap. I know what you want."

"Look, I'm not Mr. Wassermann. He's upstairs. And between you and me, I don't think he's Jewish. My name is George."

"You can call yourself anything you like."

"What's your name?"

"Simone."

George fumbled with a number of objects on the desk while Simone, stepping closer, inspected him with a degree of contempt which George found strangely exciting. He was opening his mouth to say God knows what when Magdalene came in.

"Darling, this is Simone, who's come to torture Mr. Wassermann and make him pay for it. How like marriage it is."

"Good," said Magdalene to Simone. "I'll take you upstairs."

"We'll have a drink later, then," called George. "We've never had prostitutes, but you'll certainly find us worldly. Please make yourself at home. No one's getting out of here for days. I've been listening to the radio."

"Nice place," said Simone, sarcastically, climbing the stairs.

"We were just thinking about burning it down," said Magdalene, and rapped at Mr. Wassermann's door.

"Come Ing," said Mr. Wassermann.

Tim the Criminal

Tim still had every dime of the money. His rental of a safe-deposit box was simply a sign of his adaptation to his interesting new circumstances. He may not have had a criminal mind, but again, he had a very good one. If asked for the money, in some highly improbable situation in which he was found and threatened by Mr. Castro, he would say that the money was in *safe deposit*—and exhibit the key. Thus, he could not be killed. Rather, he would have to be allowed to enter the bank personally: and then he would call the police. Bingo! Jesus Castro cuffed and stuffed, glowering malignantly, guilty of everything in the world, Tim crying in court that he had been forced to hide drug money and only wanted his life back, and so forth.

Tim found this business of being a criminal incredibly satisfying. He was *good* at it, by all appearances, and you couldn't say it wasn't lucrative. He counted the money again and checked his pistol. He unloaded it and dum-dummed the bullets, cutting deep stars into the soft lead noses of the cartridges with a penknife. He reloaded the clip, chambered a shell, and put the cocked pistol in the drawer of the nightstand, on top of the Gideons' Bible. This, as far as Tim was concerned, was living—something he'd never really done before. Neither had anyone he knew.

The problems of his generation were thorny. There

hadn't been any war, to make people grow up (wars make you do that—hardly anything else does), and no one got married, either. Nothing happened. Nobody tried to kill you—you couldn't starve—the jobs were all stupid—there was no revolution. If you couldn't get hanged or killed, Tim thought, what was the point of getting up in the morning? People were condemned to adolescence until well into their thirties, as far as Tim could tell, after which they would attempt last-ditch to simulate maturity, only to be thwarted by senescence. Tim had thought about things considerably, and he realized that what he was doing now, via the stolen money, was checking out of the whole fucking thing. Tim Picasso was checking out of his generation. He was checking out of the century. He was checking out of *history*.

If you have enough money you can live in any century you like, Tim thought, and despite affection for the nineteenth (Tim would have adored living in 1805, swigging opium, brooding in towers, scrambling up crags in a cloak), what he really wanted to do was to live in his own idea of the next one. That was the grand idée behind the theft of the money. He realized that it was entirely possible that if he invested very carefully he might be able to buy an uninhabited island, maybe a town, or even a small country by the age of forty. Or, on the other hand, he could buy a compound and not let people in unless they could pass an intelligence test. This was not misanthropy—Tim didn't have a misanthropic bone in his body—it was an interest in personal *survival*. Tim had lived in America, all his life: now what he wanted was happiness—and sanity, if there was any going around.

What was Jesus Castro's money *for*? What was *money*

for, anyway? Tim had very little idea. Tim was not good with money. Tim was essentially and profoundly the sort of man who in another age would have been signing lordlike for saddles and serfs, with money that, also lordlike, he did not have. In short, you might say, he had always behaved like or been a wealthy person who found himself temporarily out of money. Without a massive preliminary infusion of cash, he'd obviously get into trouble with landlords and police-men and ex-wives and that sort of thing (you had to look ahead), while he was wandering around thinking Noble Thoughts; and *that* was what Jesus Castro's money was for: a prophylactic against hurting other people . . . doing things like forcing his grandmother to do janitorial work so Tim could drink coffee, think about the nature of the uni-verse, and occasionally revamp the Pietà.

If you weren't independent, Tim thought, not only did you hurt other people, you got it in the neck yourself. You had to get a job—and try to be an artist simultaneously. How the fuck did you do that? Tim imagined having to try to slip something Giocondan into a magazine layout or an adver-tisement for running shoes—staggering home to a walkup from a job cleaning carpets—getting beaten up in the For-eign Legion or something. It wasn't the same as slipping good stuff into a standard Senecan revenging. A job? That was no way to be an artist. Tim knew instinctively, and bet-ter than he knew anything else, that the artist operated in one way and one way only: you got a pile of money, you lived on it judiciously in order to produce your work; you got an-other pile of money, and did the same thing, and so on, until you were dead and stray pilgrims came once a year and poured cognac on your tombstone—or pissed on it.

Being an artist was completely different from being like other people. It wasn't *better*. It was simply completely different. That was the first thing you had to realize. You needed a pile of money. If nobody would give you one (Dr. Locarno, Lorenzo the Magnificent, your dad), or you didn't get one by accident, you were on your own. Which is to say, dead. Asking someone like Tim to get a job and to *pay attention* to it was like asking a chimp to fry eggs. It wasn't possible. So essentially, Tim's thought was: *Fuck* Jesus Castro. And fuck Dr. Locarno, too. Tim was going to put the money into an account in Andorra, and live in Paris, Rome . . . Toledo, even . . . and anyone who didn't like it could fuck off. Or get killed, for that matter, if it came to it. Tim also realized with peculiar clarity something else Dr. Locarno would never know: that an artist was in no way a citizen, and that it was best to get that straight at the beginning.

There was a knock at the door. Tim forgot that he was a criminal, and went and opened it incautiously. Magdalene leaped on him and propelled him backward onto the bed, which still had about ten thousand dollars strewn all over it.

"I knew you were perfect," she cried.

"The door's open."

"You told George! That was genius."

"He asked. I have a problem with honesty."

"It was brilliant. Why don't people ever think of honesty? What is it with all this creeping around, the threats . . . the *searching* through purses . . ."

"Look, Magdalene, stop that for a minute, I have to tell you something."

"Oh-oh," said Magdalene.

Tim disentangled himself and stood up. "Don't misunderstand me. The only people obligated to respect marriages are the people in them. If you don't respect your marriage it would be presumptuous of me to do so. So this is not my point. But the fact is, I wanted a quiet hotel, not a ménage."

"Do you honestly think that I'm procuring you for George?"

"That's not what 'ménage' means."

Magdalene stared at him blankly.

"You mean a ménage à trois. This is a ménage . . . with three people in it."

Tim gave up and went to fix himself a drink.

"George doesn't care. It's not as if he's Sicilian."

"It's the men who don't care, supposedly, who suddenly appear with a fire ax."

"You've done this before?"

"Sicilians are at least predictable. They mainly break kitchen appliances and punch their wives. The largest part of the Italian culture—the business of being Italian—is doing exactly what Italians are expected to do, so you can say, 'Well, I'm Italian,' and get away with almost anything. Either murder, or farting in a singlet."

"You've done this before."

"You're missing the point."

"Are you breaking it off?"

"What?" said Tim, looking at her over his glass of whiskey.

"I asked, are you breaking it off?"

From the next room, there was a hoarse male cry, as if

someone had been kicked in the genitals, and then a sound of chains being slowly manipulated, as if Fortunato were dangling in the crypt.

"What the hell is *that*?" asked Tim.

"Mr. Wassermann has a guest," Magdalene said flatly.

There was an unmistakable sound of ferocious—positively naval—flogging. Tim went to the wall, pressed his ear against it, and listened. For an instant, he thought he heard a muffled cry in Spanish. But this was surely impossible. He went and poured another drink, and drank it, peering out at the snow. Tim eventually realized defocusedly, open-mouthed, that Magdalene had been talking to him for some time.

"—and suddenly, I don't know, I feel alive again. Of course, it might be the sex. But I think it's more than that. I really do."

"Well, it's never just the sex," said Tim lectorially (he was, after all, twenty-two). "But it's never much of anything more."

"What a fucking awful thing to say."

"It's strictly biological," Tim insisted. "Look, the basic reason you're interested in me sexually is that I'd have good-looking children and I look like I could pay for them, and if it came to it, kill enemies. I'm sick of this shit where people don't admit that they are mating. Like mynah birds or badgers. I was just thinking about this. We don't admit we're mating. Nobody ever gets married, so we don't know what we're doing anymore."

"I married George, and he couldn't kill anyone."

"I think we could pinpoint the sensations of 'love' as

being mainly those of intense and most importantly *novel* sexual arousal."

"Novel? What has it got to do with fiction?"

"Everything," said Tim, because, unexpectedly, it did. "But that phenomenon passes."

"It did with George."

"Precisely! And why?"

"Because he doesn't have any money?" asked Magdalene, trying to get into the spirit of things.

"No, no, it would pass anyway. It always passes. That's why there are lingerie stores, and Caribbean islands, and booze." Tim took a drink. "So people can lie to themselves."

"You're not making sense."

"Oh, but I am," said Tim. "Anyway, don't go around talking about loving anyone until they have a colostomy bag and no teeth or money. I'm not saying that pure love cannot exist: it's just that I've never seen it, and therefore I am obligated to take the agnostic position."

"Don't you *fucking* look at me," screamed a woman's voice next door.

"If I were a penniless cripple from Tierra del Fuego, and you said you loved me, then we could talk."

"I haven't said—"

Magdalene, glancing at the money, realized that if she continued, she might be disastrously misinterpreted. Something smashed next door and a man screamed in pain.

"*That's* nice," said Tim, indicating the wall with his drink. "Of course, nothing I'm saying about biology applies to people like that."

"I know what I want out of life," said Magdalene abruptly.

"Pray continue," said Tim.

"What you actually want out of life," said Magdalene very slowly, suffused with the internal glow of the philosopher, "is the last thing you ever admit. I'm going to change all that."

"Universally?" asked Tim, intrigued.

"Yes, with everyone! They'll see how wonderful and right I am, and beat a path to my door. I've always known that would happen, but I was never sure how. Here goes." Magdalene took a deep breath. "I want to have money, and go out to lunch a lot. I want to shop, and I want people to think I'm pretty."

"That's it?"

"If I wanted to be abused verbally," said Magdalene, "I'd call my father."

"Or you could go next door." Tim poured another whiskey.

"Don't you understand the courage I just displayed? I'm a modern American woman, and I just admitted that I'm a complacent, unambitious, shallow, and selfish dipshit. Some of us are! I'm the first one who ever said it! It was me! Me!" She threw money into the air.

"You could have a church."

"Yes!" said Magdalene.

"We're all dipshits!" said Tim. "That's the whole point. We're worms crawling on the earth. Well, it's certainly a day for it, anyway. I just admitted to myself that I am essentially a sociopath. In twentieth-century terms, anyway, which don't really matter anymore. If what was a king in the twelfth century was, in the twentieth, Charles Manson, what

the fuck are we dealing with, anyway? I've also been thinking something else. May I digress?"

"What?" asked Magdalene.

"All these problems people have. Relative to the rest of
the world," said Tim, peering through cigarette smoke, and
getting toward a thought, "the American middle class—
that is, people like us—have no real problems. But there's a
fault in this. Because you see, human beings need a certain
amount of drama. Therefore problems are made up. Let me
tell you something about this century, Magdalene. It's no
accident that Freud emerged with the rise of leisure."

"Is that what he did?" asked Magdalene warily.

"He wasn't actually commenting on the discontents of
civilization. He was marketing new forms of discontent to
the civilized."

"I can see that." Magdalene was unconvincing.

"It's very major," said Tim, and after pouring another
drink he went to the escritoire, where he did what you do at
an escritoire, and wrote something down.

Chapter 20

Mr. Whistler Versus the Elements

Lucille, puffing, lifted Mr. Whistler from his wheelchair and put him into the backseat of his car. She arranged a blanket over his legs. George bent down at the open door. There were snowflakes in his eyelashes. Visibility was zero. The cannonade of surf sent spray flying overhead, and the wind was keening and terrible. Still, George shouted cordially at Mr. Whistler.

"Thank you again, Mr. Whistler, for your patronage. Tea would not be the same without you."

"Wouldn't be anybody," shouted Lucille. "Tea my ass."

Lucille's hat blew off. She put Mr. Whistler's wheelchair into the trunk. George fetched Lucille's hat from the snow.

"Look, we really do have tea. You're being very difficult."

"Tea my ass," Lucille repeated.

"Best of luck with the barium thing!" George hollered at Mr. Whistler. Mr. Whistler stared at George dumbly as Lucille struggled behind the wheel of the car, then put it with a jerk into gear. It reversed, turned, and disappeared immediately into the blizzard. George went back into the inn. In the main parlor, he added logs to the fire. Above the sound of surf and wind, he became aware of the unmistakable sound, from the Easterly Room, of what was technically called fornication. He looked slowly up at the ceiling.

"Christ," said George. He went and got a drink. After a moment, he convinced himself that Tim was doing calisthenics. Maybe he had a few other people up there, too, and an elephant. Cheered, George went and looked, or tried to look, out of a snow-plastered seaward window. The lighthouse (which George knew was definitely there—like God, say, or his marriage) was again invisible in the storm. Poor Mr. Briscoe, he thought. Then he thought: Fucking pinhead.

The sounds from the room above became violent, and George, in a stroke of glazed genius, decided that a shutter was banging, loudly and repeatedly, and ever faster. He went upstairs and opened the door to the Easterly Room. Then he closed the door and stood reflectively in the hall. He was not exactly sure what he had seen. It *could* have been his wife clinging to a juddering headboard, looking like an even less literate Saint Teresa of Ávila, but it *could* have been something else . . . something other than it seemed. . . . Yes. Some destructive hallucination perpetrated on him by some recreant Iago-god . . . (or *Negro Bakerman?*) . . . who . . . lived in the attic or something, and had a hologram machine. (Mr. Glowery, now wandering in the blizzard trying the wrong doors of the hotel, would have instantly detected the hand of *John Wong*; George's intellect, perhaps unfortunately, had no such apparatus). After a few moments, in a spirit of scientific curiosity, George opened the door again. He started to speak, gave it up as a bad idea, closed the door with a precise click, and spun on his heel and fainted in the hallway.

Lying half-conscious and cruciform on the floor,

George thought about how very satisfying it was to faint: one could lie there powerlessly: it was comfortable. There was a reason it had always been a powerful refuge of the corseted powerless. He was surprised it hadn't made a comeback. While he was lying there thinking these things, he heard the bathroom door click, and he slowly opened his eyes. Inches away from his right eye was a small black shoe with a spiked heel. Then another shoe. George looked hesitantly higher, and a pair of slender legs in black fishnet stockings came into view. Simone, in a black leather bustier, stood looking down impassively but not unpleasantly at George. Her short blond hair was mussed, and in her hand she held what appeared to be a hood with a zipper.

"What are you doing on the floor?" she asked.

George scrambled affably to his feet. "Epilepsy," he said, and knocked a small painting off the wall. "Grand mal."

"I know an epileptic," said Simone. "She makes big money."

"Yes," cried Magdalene from the Easterly Room.

"Some people are sick," said George defensively.

"Some people like donuts," said Simone, matter-of-factly.

"To make an analogy to outré sex," said George, who had a bottle, "you would have to say they *like liking* donuts. It's not the same thing as *liking* them. There's always a chance you mainly want to be *seen* liking something. It's not the same as liking it. The world is a whirlwind of seeming."

Simone stared at George. George revised his manner,

and became obsequious, rather than kitchen-philosophical, and distrait.

"Everything all right?"

"I need a fucking cigarette."

"Downstairs," said George.

"I'll come down," said Simone. "I need a break."

Descending the stairs, Simone looked at him with an incuriosity that in anyone else would have been an expression of quasi-medical alarm. George was emotionally wrecked and his hair was sticking up.

"You know," said George, brightening, "I find the whole idea of what you do rather fascinating. My taste in sex has always been what you'd call 'vanilla.'"

"So what," said Simone.

"Well, I never thought about your sort of thing before, but since we've been chatting I find myself thinking about it almost constantly. In theory, no rational human wants to get tortured by an antagonist and then *maybe* be allowed to masturbate into the garbage if he pays more money, but recently I have recognized a basic similarity between this and my marriage."

"I thought you were gay."

"No. This is a speech impediment."

"What about that sweater?"

George looked down at his cardigan.

Simone said nothing.

"Obviously I'll never have normal sex again, after what I just saw upstairs," George continued. "I perceive a long period of that sort of sexual supercaution which can be gratuitously read as impotence. It's ungallant to admit that you don't want to fuck your wife, even if she's a monster. That's where this 'impotence' thing comes from. Men sit there in doctors' offices saying anything but the truth. Don't tell anybody I told you this."

It conflicted so utterly with anything Simone knew about anything (she had not been a prostitute for very long) that she hadn't even heard it anyway.

"Under the circumstances, I think I ought to consider some sexual variation, don't you? Something out-of-character is fine. My character may be out of character. What I'm saying is that I'd feel better about this whole thing if I at least saw another woman naked—even if it was in the split second before she killed me. Do a lot of your clients use martyrological metaphor?"

"Maybe," said Simone.

"You know, only this morning," said George, chuckling, "I thought of Magdalene as a cross to bear."

"I just want a cigarette," said Simone.

"What does it feel like to be flogged, I wonder."

"Flogged?"

"Beaten. Whipped."

"*I* don't know."

"Of course. You—"

"Yes."

George stared at her ravenously and then ducked behind the desk and came up with a package of cigarettes. Simone took one. George lit a wooden match, which cracked and exploded, and then with jittering hands offered another, which burned his fingers.

"So," said George, "what *is* your own sexual . . . whatever."

"None of your beeswax."

"It's a point of simple curiosity," protested George. "We're here to learn. Pointlessly. That's what the world's all about. I think."

Simone boredly exhaled. "I'm a treatment queen."

"Which is—?"

"I like men to jack off in my hair."

"I see. Oh my God. Christ. I see. Wow. Look—"

The door blew open and one snowman came in carrying another. After a moment, George recognized Lucille and Mr. Whistler.

"Good God."

"Motherfucking car went off the motherfucking road," Lucille finally managed to say.

"Oh dear," said George.

"Tits," said Mr. Whistler, weakly. He scrabbled at Simone as he was carried past her.

"You hush up," said Lucille, to Mr. Whistler, glaring at Simone.

"Take him into the parlor," said George, baronially.

The old man was carried through the door and set down on a sofa, which George moved closer to the fire. Lucille whipped off Mr. Whistler's porkpie hat and threw it across the room. Then she wrestled him violently out of his overcoat. Mr. Whistler was blue around the mouth and looked feverish. "Tits?" he repeated hopefully.

George, at a loss, poured him a sherry. "A rather amusing rotgut Amontillado," he said. "Let's all have one."

"This shit out there be dangerous," said Lucille. "Snow, gnome seign, shit. Ain't no day out there for man or beast. Motherfucker go by in a plow with a yellow light. I say yo! I got an old white man dying here gnome seign, but *he* don't stop, yellow-light plow-ass motherfucker. Shit. Gimme some of that." Lucille took a belt of sherry. The pompom of her hat bobbed. She looked malevolently at Simone, who, in an entirely out-of-character way, was rubbing Mr. Whistler's cold hands.

"It was in Paris before the war," said Mr. Whistler, in a strange autobiographical tone, "that I commenced my erotic education."

"I told you that trash bitch work the old man up. He like that girl give the weather on TV, too."

"Tits," said Mr. Whistler in the final agony.

"Shut up you old motherfucker! I put you in the snow."

Jesus Castro unexpectedly entered the room just then, wearing a voluminous bathrobe with padded shoulders, a huge cigar in his mouth. George looked at him with bleak politesse.

"Lucille, Simone, Mr. Whistler—may I present Mr. Wassermann."

Everyone stared at Jesus Castro.

"I feel relax," said Jesus Castro. "Hey, look the damn snow!"

"It's a three-day blow," said George. "A nor'easter."

Jesus Castro was in a very good mood, having actually been relaxed twice. He puffed at his cigar, then removed the Havana from his lips. "Hey you guy," he said to George. "Where some thing to eat some tine?"

"In light of the storm, I thought of serving corn chowder, salmon, and peas."

Jesus Castro stared at George.

"It's what we have up here on the Fourth of July."

"You get me some nice Chinese food."

"Chinese food," George repeated.

Cigar in mouth, Jesus Castro peeled two hundred-dollar bills off a roll he produced from his bathrobe pocket, and slapped them into George's palm. "Some for everybody. Find out what everybody like. Twenty bucks for you. Get enough. Too much, we eat it cold later, you know what I min. Hey I like this place. I feel relax." He shrugged like a boxer and then stood happily by the fireplace, distractedly fellating his soaked cigar. He turned and saw George standing vacantly in the middle of the room.

"Hey. You guy. I don't see no fucking Chinese."

"Well, the driving's pretty bad, Mr. Wassermann."

"So they deliver these to me. Whassa matta with you."

Jesus Castro noticed Mr. Whistler lying moribund on the couch, and stood staring at him for some time.

"That guy don' look so good," said Jesus Castro.

"Well, as a matter of fact," said George, "Mr. Whistler's car went off the road, and he and his servant—"

"What the *fuck* you say?" shouted Lucille.

"—nearly didn't get back here alive. So as you see, conditions are pretty ghastly."

"Whatever," said Jesus Castro. "So no Chinese food. Okay. No Chinese food." But he looked so bitter about it that George had an attack of innkeeper's agony, and he went to the phone box in the lobby. There was Magdalene, sitting on a parson's bench and crying.

"You had sex with Mr. Picasso *again*."

"I did not!"

"Magdalene. I *saw* you. You were holding the head-board and screaming."

Magdalene said nothing for a moment.

"I want to get away from you," said Magdalene, "but everyone else wants to get away from me."

"You *are* a bit clingy," said George.

"I hate you." She blew her nose. "I really, really, really hate you."

"Will you kindly make yourself useful? I think Mr. Whistler is dying. I'm sure he could use a cup of fucking tea. Good Lord. The phone's dead."

It was, too, but not for the obvious wind-and-snow reasons. What had happened was that the Tyburn Taxi containing the half-conscious Mr. Glowery had slammed into the telephone pole at the end of the causeway and toppled it into the sea. Mr. Glowery had managed to stagger to the inn, but mistook the side stairs for the front entrance, and was at present dying of exposure while pulling weakly at a locked French door.

"I don't want it to hurt you, George," said Magdalene, "but I'm in love with Tim Picasso."

"Oh, nonsense. You want it to be an unspeakable agony. Well, it isn't. I've got my own interests, you know. I've been having an affair for years."

"With *whom*," demanded Magdalene.

George, at a loss, said, "That tall woman who runs the frame shop."

"She's a lesbian separatist."

"That's what *you* think."

"*I've* had sex with her, George."

"That is neither here nor there. I may not be fucking a lesbian separatist, at least regularly, but I'm not an unattractive man. There are some very bad things about me, but I intend to have them savagely corrected."

"Why are you putting on your coat?"

"That Hispanic monster wants Chinese food, and if I can't get him any, he'll probably murder us all. Wait. Perhaps I can combine trips! Obviously Mr. Whistler has to go to the hospital. So I'll drop him off at the hospital," George concluded feverishly, "and then pop round the Luau Dragon."

"I never had an orgasm with you, George."

"Good, we're even, then," said George, and tottered back into the parlor.

"This place ain' bad," Jesus Castro was saying to the comatose Mr. Whistler. "Got character. Good place for a guy like me to come relax. A little business, a little pleasure, you know what I min?"

Mr. Whistler's eyes had rolled back in his head.

"Me personally I'm a guy works all the time. Look at that shit." Mr. Castro had gestured, with wet cigar, to the bad reproduction of Winslow Homer's *Breezing Up*, which hung above the fireplace.

"That's some good shit. You ever see him engravings? Not exactly my taste. I go for the abstract. You know de Kooning? I got him. Big one. Yellow, red, this way, that way, don' know what the fuck's going on. Art, to me, is mystery. You *know* what happen—is no good. You gotta sit there and think yourself, What the fuck is these say to me? Then you got Art. You know what I'm say?"

This unexpected monologue threw everyone into a state

of admiration for Jesus Castro, who sat down complacently in a chair by the fireplace and replaced his cigar in his mouth.

"Better throttle these baby in these thing they sleep in, some tie," added Jesus Castro. "That nurse the Unacted Desire. Is a guy say that."

Chapter 21

Mr. Briscoe Triumphant

Mr. Briscoe, adrift, had expected to die. But he did not die. He did not freeze to death and he was not bashed into particles of fish food and shredded survival suit on the jagged rocks of the mainland. Instead, riding the storm tide like a spider toward a drain, he had been *swept around* the inn's black headland and into the anchorage cove under the warmly lit (and from this perspective vaguely castellate) Admiral Benbow. Floating inertly in the water, his face frozen, Mr. Briscoe wept with relief.

Fuckin' A, thought Mr. Briscoe.

The water was still calm in the cove, the breakwater having held. The temperature of the water was about twelve degrees Fahrenheit, but compared with what Mr. Briscoe had been through *outside* the cove, the water in the cove had almost a tropical balminess. On the stone jetty not fifty feet away, his beloved building materials were stacked cozily under snow-whitened tarpaulins—the lights of the inn shone above—and Mr. Briscoe, in the absolute extremity of absolute joy, saw that the tide was sweeping him straight toward the banjaxed work float below the jetty. Mr. Briscoe coughed seawater, and splashed weakly. He had been very plainly given a second chance by God, who wanted him to wear women's clothing—perhaps just at home in the beginning, but later on, who knew? Mr. Briscoe, a man of plain faith, could plainly recognize the workings of an intelligent Providence.

The current carried him well inside the breakwater, and slowly past the scarred hull of his own lobster boat. Ten yards farther on toward the jetty, though, his progress was mysteriously arrested. Water slopped into his face, which would have expressed alarm if it had not already been frozen into a mottled vizard of the same expression, permanently modeled in blackening, ice-crystallized flesh. After a moment of dazed consternation, Mr. Briscoe realized that some sort of strap dangling from the leg of his Swedish survival suit had of all things caught fast on part of the rigging of George's sunken sloop, the *Anglia*, which had been resting on the bottom of the cove for two years, occasionally releasing a burp of diesel fuel and rotted paperbacks.

Mr. Briscoe, despite a life spent largely at sea, had an irrational horror of sunken boats, which was instantly activated. Not only could he see the *Anglia*'s dark rotting specter beneath him in the water, he could sense it. Furthermore, he was caught on it. For a moment, the tide dragging at him, he was merely hurt and confused; slightly disappointed; but then he started to struggle and scream. The storm tide continued to rise, and Mr. Briscoe, caught on the rigging of the *Anglia*, remained at the same level.

Ficciones

Professor Menelaus Eggman had not been up against it, or at least not for very long. No more than fifteen minutes after being hurled into the road by the cabdriver, he was hauled out of a snowdrift by a local brute with a pointed bald head. Archy Lafata, his evil at first undetectable in an anorak, bundled the now yeti-like and also unidentifiable professor into the passenger seat of a burbling Chevy Malibu with a metronome tick of blown cylinders, and drove him straight to the Admiral Benbow, where Professor Eggman had a seminar to conduct and Archy expected to retrieve his pirate.

Professor Eggman clawed his way up the steps into the inn. At this point Archy Lafata threw the car into reverse and found himself irretrievably stuck. He got out of his car and unfolded a small portable shovel, which instantly broke in half when he tried to dig it into the snow. He had just thrown the bits away when he saw Mr. Glowery staggering irresolutely through the snowdrifts at the side of the inn. Archy Lafata was a first-things-first kind of guy, and he figured he'd better have his car ready after he retrieved his pirate, and the pirate didn't look like he was much good at the moment for digging or pushing things, so he left him alone, and stuck, as God intended, to his labor.

Professor Eggman entered the inn, and after peering vaguely into the parlor, where a huge Hispanic man fallen to his knees was being brutalized by an ear-twisting woman in leather, he went along through the seaward rooms toward the billiards room, where, he feared, his poor remaining students had been attempting to solve fiction without his special insights. Actually what he found was Saraswati sleeping on a sofa, and Joel Josh O'Connor reading his mandatory copy of *The Best Short Stories in the History of the World*. Professor Menelaus Eggman, his head still adorned with a busby of snow, made an inarticulate noise, raised a palm, and then in search of hot drink went to the kitchen, where a voluptuous woman—vaguely connected in some servile way to the appalling inn—was intoxicating herself privily with cheap Spanish wine.

"The storm," said Professor Eggman, "is ferocious. Spray is flying over the roof. Are you sure we're safe here?"

"Physically," said Magdalene.

"What does that mean?" asked the professor.

"I'm very busy," said Magdalene. "I'm not here to define everything for you."

"The building is *shaking*."

"This house," said Magdalene loftily, "has been here since 1888."

This was not exactly true. The *estate* had survived nor'easters, as a piece of physical property, and so had *parts* of the house, but little of the house was original. In the past the sea had carted away the wreckage of gazebos, innumerable porches, and seven or eight boathouses and sheds. An Arts and Crafts cottage had lasted less than three days after completion, and had been dragged off the headland in 1927, containing Mrs. Thomas G. Amberville, the opiated lesbian authoress of *My God, Your God, Is in the Garden*.

"May I have some tea?" asked Professor Eggman.

"Certainly," said Magdalene. "You have infinite choice in the realm of nature."

"Thank you. Will you kindly bring it into the billiards room?"

"Why don't you go in there," said Magdalene, "and see if I do."

"Thank you," said Professor Eggman, and took his leave.

The members of the Fiction Workshop had been carefully chosen by the Professor for their intense, if not morbid, seriousness about Fiction. Not one of the twelve had committed a single witticism in any of his writing samples. This is what Seriousness is all about. It had been a prime crop of twelve, too: not a single one of them doubting that a short story was a picture of life *in which something almost but did not quite happen*—this traditional lack of incident invariably resulting in what in the trade was known—

traditionally—as an *epiphany*. Because of the inclemency of the weather, as we are aware, only two of the workshoppers had actually arrived at the Admiral Benbow; but they were perfectly representative. Joel Josh O'Connor was a writer of moderate technical gift who was capable of imitating everything, no matter how various in style (which does not, week to week, denote uncommon range), that he had read in the last issue of *The New Yorker*. Careers have been made of less: far less: Professor Eggman had high hopes for Master O'Connor. Which is to say, he hoped, highly, that Mr. O'Connor would not be published in *The New Yorker* before he was. Saraswati for her part was "issues"-driven, with a profound passion for everything unrelated to her own upbringing and environment. Her prose, and worse, was generally about someone sitting in Bumbwanda or something, covered with flies, eating porridge from a sock, and thinking about things in complete English sentences. She had won several awards.

Such artists were Professor Eggman's meat and potatoes, and mercifully there were enough of them. There being only two, here, now, had its advantages: Professor Eggman enjoyed the chance to give young writers individual and styptic attention. It meant less work, too. As far as the money went, the steepish fees paid by the missing ten persons were, of course, nonrefundable. There was another advantage in the decimation of the workshop: there was less of a chance that a writer would hang himself in his room (as had happened to Professor Eggman before), or burst into dreadful riot when someone in all innocence and a spirit of helpfulness called someone else's writing "clenched" or "turgid" without knowing what either thing actually meant—which at writing workshops invariably happens.

Professor Eggman knew what could happen if you got the wrong people in a fiction workshop, and he chose his candidates very carefully. You were best off with women in workshops because the males tended to fight with one another like rut-crazed pronghorn antelope, giving the erroneous impression that human endeavor is about sexual competition. (Which it is.) So you chose women who desired to write about their "issues," and threw in one or two males of the gentler and more controllable variety.

If you injected a quart of sodium pentothal directly into Professor Eggman's brain stem you might have a thirty-percent chance of having him tell you that talent was not very big on Professor Eggman's shrewd, or shrewdish, selections agenda. Whenever Professor Menelaus Eggman came across anyone with original talent, he threw the manuscript into the trash, where it belonged, both for private reasons and in the interest of feelings and good order. And this wasn't a bad thing: talent's place is in the market, and Professor Eggman was happy to let it be extinguished there, as it usually was—except of course when it flourished and made people feel bad about themselves. Professor Eggman provided a service: a literary workshop was for people of goodwill and considerable limitations who needed a *safe space* in which they could explore their fantasies of talent. It was like baseball camp. People were willing to pay for this sort of thing, and Professor Eggman was willing to take their money. All of it, if they insisted.

"Right then," the professor said, removing his hat, and wondering with racist élan if Mr. O'Connor (who had been waiting quite a while, and was lying on the floor) was perfectly sober. He went to the chalkboard he had set up and wrote one of his truisms:

CHARACTERS ARE EITHER GOOD OR EVIL

Then, as if someone had grabbed his hand, he wrote:

I AM LIVING IN A MATERIAL WORLD
AND I AM A MATERIAL GIRL

"Disregard this," said Professor Eggman stentoriously.

Meanwhile, brooding by his fire in the Easterly Room, Tim Picasso tossed away a complimentary tide-chart that told him that high tide would come in three hours. He began to wonder whether, after all, he had done the right thing to steal the money, even though he'd just convinced himself that he not only had been right but had pioneered a whole new mode of existence. It made perfect sense (money! take it, buy things), but being a New Englander, and essentially Wittenbergian (which is the same thing as being a New Englander, but fancier), he had reneged on his wingéd insight and was with dark comfort numbering his considerable flaws.

This was the world: it was ridiculous to think that doing something reasonable would result in something reasonable. He had made a rational decision to steal drug money, and where had it gotten him? Exactly where each and every one of his other major—and a lot of the minor—decisions had gotten him—into an indecorous affair with a woman with mental problems. There was a possibility that he had already died and was in hell, condemned to repeat himself endlessly no matter how novel and inspired or logical any action or decision seemed to be. He could go to the Amazon—he could become a gambler in Kowloon—he could become a professor of history, a novelist, an astronaut, a Jesuit, or even, through surgical procedure, a woman, but he would without question end up in an indecorous affair with a woman with mental problems. A less sophisticated man—like Archy Lafata, for example, the least sophisticated person on earth—would simply say that Tim thought with his dick, but Tim had an education and various other privileges, and privilege is about nothing so much as gratuitous and enjoyable confusion. Tim poured himself a whiskey and stared into the fire.

"I am callow, and unproductive," said Tim aloud.

The wind seemed for an instant to contain a wild human scream.

Tim buckled in and really started enjoying himself. "I am disrespectful of my own gifts. Having genius is a kind of a hobby, not a profession. Dr. Locarno was right. Art is not about talent, but sincerity, and crude single-mindedness. Who am I to have a gnawing sense that every art form is too small? I sleep too late in the morning. I've always been good-looking, and now I have too much money. I'm doomed."

The idea of confession became strangely appealing. He had to confess something—anything, really—to anyone available. Even if he had to make something up. As someone who had been raised Catholic, he had no particular problem with this. At the age of six Tim had told a priest that he had lit his cat on fire, and had ended up in analysis despite the fact—and then because of the fact—that he had no cat at all. Tim had deeply Catholic instincts, and being an atheist presented many difficulties, not the least of which was that he had, specious and enjoyable claims of immorality aside, never done anything really immoral. So on the whole it was a rather good thing that Tim had, by stealing the money, procured for himself an authentic Sin—a cloud of actual guilt—a fear of entirely possible retribution. Jesus Castro as a vindictive god was rather a small deity in a closed system, but it was a relief to finally have a recognizable universe, and if it turned out, after all, to be a false cosmogony, so be it. All the rest were.

Jesus Castro was dozing in his chair by the fire, a copy of *Boys' Life* resting on his paunch, dreaming about building an airplane in his garage. Mr. Briscoe was about ready to give up the ghost as the tide rose above his ears. Tim, now on his eleventh whiskey, was in his room, imagining a film set in a seaside hotel in winter. Film was obviously the way to go, for a guy like Tim, for was it not the art that contained all the others? (He was well launched into hubris again, thank God, after a brief vacation in self-doubt.) Magdalene was in the kitchen talking to Simone, who was waiting for a break in the monologue to tell Magdalene that she'd asked for a tampon, not Magdalene's life story.

Mr. Glowery was pulling weakly at the locked door of a seaward porch, and occasionally trying to light a match from Veruka, a New York boîte where he had recently been for a "film meeting" of the sort that torments writers like Mr. Glowery, who happen to be unaware that film people meet with *everybody*, no matter how little their business actually depends on personal contact, simply to manage to eat and get drunk using the company credit card. It's part of their *pay*, but they need *you* to get it. Journalism had been as kind to Mr. Glowery: he was the sort of damaged marginal that the magazines troll for in catch-and-release experiments. Mr. Glowery, however, was convinced that his memoir was nearly in glittering production and that Mr. Glowery himself would soon enough be regarding from seigneurial altitude a jasmine-scented canyon, the lights of Los Angeles spread before him like jewelry spilled on the cloak of a king whose name was probably Glowery.

What else was going on? Archy Lafata was digging out his car. Professor Eggman was Professor Eggman, and there was very little doubt about that. Mr. Whistler was dead, and George was explaining this to the people at the emergency room.

Chapter 23

Mr. Whistler Kicks the Bucket

Well it's a terrible shock," said George. "All of a sudden he just . . . *died*. I'm sure it's my fault somehow."

"Not at all," said the intern. "He had advanced pulmonary edema, severe congestion of the heart, emphysema,

Alzheimer's disease, and cancer of the pancreas. He was ninety-seven years old."

"Right. I suppose the police will come around, though."

"Not at all."

George had a masochistic twinge of disappointment. The fluorescent lights buzzed overhead.

"If you're sure—"

"Thank you for bringing him in, Mr. Hawthorne. I'd say you'd better get home while you can."

"Why?" asked George, quickly.

"There's a nor'easter," said the intern.

"Oh! I thought you were talking about the police."

"No, I was talking about the snow."

"Ever since I was a child," said George, "I've thought that everything was my fault, and that I would pay some great penalty in the end. Do you have a psychiatric ward?"

"Would you like to talk to someone?"

"No, no, no," George recovered himself. "Rugged individualism. That's my personal cup of tea. Always has been. I'm not the sort of man who finds himself shattered by the death of a customer. My wife's leaving me, of course, and I'm not an artist, and I'm having sadomasochistic fantasies. But I'm all right, really. Life goes on. In its dubious splendor."

". . . Yes, Mr. Hawthorne, I suppose it does."

"No it *doesn't*. Look at Mr. Whistler. There's a sheet over his face!"

"That's because he's dead."

"That's what I'm talking about. Let me ask you something. As a doctor. Do you ever look at people and see their skulls?"

"The ward you were asking about is down there—your second left, past the Coke machine."

"I've tried therapy. Do you know what I did, on the first day? I walked in and said, Dr. Wehrmacht, I'm not an artist, my wife doesn't love me, and I think I'm insane. Do you know what that bastard said to me? He said that I was an artist, that my wife cared for me deeply, and that I was psychologically quite normal. Dr. Wehrmacht told me lies of this character every Tuesday for a year, and gave me drugs so I'd believe him. In fact, my poetry isn't avant-garde, you know. It sucks. My wife is leaving me, and I'm crazy as a fucking bedbug. So put that in your hat."

George stormed out through the automatic doors. The wind blew him into a snowdrift. He struggled out gamely, staggered through the wind, dragged himself along the side of an ambulance on top of which a tree had fallen, and got into the Volvo, which was still running, and full of heat. He put it into gear, depressed the gas pedal, and drove off.

It had really not been that difficult to get the Volvo on the road (bless the Swedes), or to keep it there. The northeast storm was so furious that the snow had tended to drift heavily against southwestern obstacles, but there was little snow anywhere else, except in the air. George, jittering, smoking one cigarette after another, drove spastically, peering forward over the wheel.

George's driving was bad, even in the best of conditions (one observer had thought of Eleanor Roosevelt playing pinball); he had no license, and the car was not insured. It slowly began to dawn on him, with the intensity of a religious vision, that he didn't give a damn about anything. "My poetry is not avant-garde. It *sucks*." He repeated this as a kind of mantra all the way through the storm to the Luau Dragon, whose neon sign glowed with a peculiar intensity in the inclement darkness.

Chapter 24

Magdalene and Jesus

Jesus Castro's dream of airplanes turned overtly sexual. He had built an airplane, but it would not take off. It had one wing, and would not fly, except in short sputtering hops as it taxied in manic circles, no matter how much the control stick was pumped—and he pumped it furiously. He woke soaked with sweat, and in a very bad mood.

"Jesus Christ," said Jesus Castro.

"You've been sleeping." Magdalene was tending the parlor fire. Jesus Castro stared at the thrusting poker with a kind of Keatsian recognizance.

"I dream I'm in an airplane. Don' take off too good."

"Does it fall from the sky?"

"Jes."

"Oh, you poor man."

"Him have one wing only and can't fly."

"George dreams of guns that fire with a flat pop, and

the bullets just sort of fall out. That's because he's frequently impotent."

"What the fuck," said Jesus Castro. He leaped to his feet. "Who you thing I am?"

Upstairs, packing, Tim flinched. The shouting voice below had sounded very familiar. Tim considered. It was impossible he had been found; but he decided that, even if he was found, there was nothing he could do about it. He couldn't kill anybody, probably. Furthermore, there was no way to get around the fact that he *had* stolen Jesus Castro's money—not hard-earned money, per se, but money representing a substantial criminal risk.

Tim felt bad about that for a moment, and quite like a thief who wanted to be caught (the Squirrel Nut incident, etc.), but then it occurred to him that if he was going to respect Jesus Castro's criminal act, it was logical that he respect his own. Beyond that, abstractly, what was money? (You had to keep asking.) *Freedom*. And whom did freedom belong to, historically? Why, the man who could keep it. Tim sat on the bed and checked his pistol.

"I go to be whip," confessed Jesus Castro, downstairs. Magdalene sat sympathetically next to him on the couch. "You tie me up—"

"And whip you?" inquired Magdalene, staring at him insolently.

"—whip me—I'm an animal. Go all night. Two tree times." He puffed his cigar happily.

Mr. Wassermann had the strangest sense of machismo Magdalene had ever encountered, if that was the word for it, which it probably wasn't.

"Well, I'm sure it's self-destructive in some way," she said.

"¿Qué?"

"Being whipped and humiliated."

"Best thing in the world," said Jesus Wassermann. "Two tree times. You know Lawrence of Arabia?"

Magdalene knew merely that Mr. Wasserman had said something incomprehensible, apparently about Arabs.

"I'm afraid I don't like Arabs. Admittedly, Mr. Wassermann, there are a lot of things wrong with radical Zionism, but I believe firmly in Israel's right to exist, and its right to cause others to cease to exist."

"¿Qué?"

"Are you Sephardic, Mr. Wassermann?"

"I go to relax." Jesus Castro, who had no idea what Magdalene had said, relit his cigar. "Hey. You tell me. There a guy here about twenny, twenny-fie, good-lookin' kid, I thing maybe I see some one like him upstair in the hall, aidonno." Jesus Castro leered cleverly at her.

Magdalene started to cry. "He's leaving tomorrow."

"I tell you secret. These guy a friend of mine. Go way back, in Miami. He don' know I'm here. But when Chinese food come, we surprise him, some time. We all get together nice, talk some business. . . . Whassa matta?"

"I'm afraid I had an affair with him."

Jesus Castro stared blankly.

"What?"

"I had an affair with him."

Jesus Castro wrestled with the concept of "affair."

"You min you fuck that guy?"

"You put it so . . . bluntly."

"Hey. Don' do that. You gonna cry? I ain' gonna hurt him."

"What do you mean, why should you hurt him?" asked Magdalene, bewilderedly.

"I just want wha's mine. What you thing I am?" Jesus Castro chuckled magnanimously. "I look like I got a gun?"

"Actually you do. Very much."

"Don' worry aboud. 'S okay. Talk business him and me over some nice Chinese, then I relax and go back to Miami in the morning. You like Miami?"

"No, of course not," said Magdalene.

Mr. Castro looked hurt. Magdalene, fretful, got up from the couch and went to the window overlooking the cove. In the storm, the window overlooked nothing, except maybe, technically, Chaos, with a capital C.

"Mr. Wassermann," said Magdalene deliberately, "let me ask you something. If I wanted to have someone killed, how would I go about it? I mean, there must be a way to do these things, and I suspect that you may know."

Jesus Castro was relieved to be able to be himself. Despite the fact that he was in his bathrobe, and incidentally named Wassermann, he became the perfect professional. He was also somewhat touched.

"Well. Good question to ask guy like me some time. First, *you thing aboud*. You thing, *you self* any way I can geddaroun kill these guy fuck with me. Number one, you don' wanna kill no one you don' have to. Some tine is no good idea, even if it seem like a good idea at the tine."

"Don't patronize me, Mr. Wassermann."

"Number *two*. You go to guy like me, Jesus Castro—"

"I thought your name was Wassermann."

"You say to me, '*Hey*, Mr. Washington, I got these fucking guy. Life is no good to me until these guy don' talk to me no more. I got these much money. Is enough you kill him.' Get me? Then I send some guys. Cost you money, maybe some thing else. Maybe money and some thing else. Maybe some thing else and more money later—but what don'?"

"Mr. Wassermann, I want my husband killed and I want this inn burned to the ground. Can we talk about it after dinner?"

Jesus Castro considered. "Your husband the guy talk funny?"

"Among other things, yes."

"Okay. I thing aboud. I give you an estimate."

Jesus Castro retired to his room to relax.

Chapter 25

A Red Shoe for Mr. Briscoe

Mr. Briscoe's predicament continued, but this predicament had ceased to interest him personally. The tide having risen, his head was underwater, and he had blacked out. When suddenly the strap of his survival suit broke free from the *Anglia*'s topmast and he bobbed like a cork to the surface, Mr. Briscoe came to consciousness with a sense not of relief, but of exhausted contempt for his circumstances. What a revoltin' development, thought Mr. Briscoe. He was apparently reprieved from death again (Providence, etc.), but by now it was difficult to give a shit.

Mr. Briscoe was washed inertly into the shallows at the end of the cove, and he crawled weakly, far gone into hypothermia, onto the rocks and broken cake ice on the snow-blasted beach. His hands were ivory claws and he could not feel his face. He would have liked to die on the beach, and in fact lay down to do it, his legs still in the water, when suddenly he had a vision.

The vision was grail-like, luminous and beautiful. What Mr. Briscoe saw, with the full attention of what remained of his mind, was a single red pump, a woman's party shoe. This vision did not come from nowhere, for Mr. Briscoe had found that very shoe in a closet of an apartment he had once renovated. He had carried it in his electrical toolbox ever since, though he had never dared to put it on. Clearly, the time had come. If the shoe fits, thought Mr. Briscoe, I'm going to wear the goddam thing.

Fortified by his new objective, Mr. Briscoe crawled whining up the beach. In a burst of perseverance, he even managed to get to his feet in the violent wind, favoring his broken arm, and slowly climbed the snow-covered steps that went up the bluff. The snow blinded him, and he was vomiting seawater, and he fell down half a dozen times, but he finally managed to get down to the jetty below the inn, where he fell whimpering through the door of his workshed. It was only after Mr. Briscoe had managed to unwrap and clutch the red pump that he thought of survival.

Sobbing, staggering, and on the verge of terminal blackout, he managed to find the light cord, and then to hit the automatic ignition switch of the shed's propane heater. It lit with a thump, incandesced, and instantly blasted hot air. Clutching the red shoe, Mr. Briscoe collapsed to the board floor of the shed—satisfied in all respects, dedicated, if he lived, to an entirely new way of life—and passed out like a clubbed haddock.

At the Sign of the Luau Dragon

"There's a big difference between what's avant-garde and what simply sucks," said George, loudly, to an elderly Chinese bartender who could not understand English, "and it pays to know the difference. My wife told me that. Hurt my feelings, at first, as you might well imagine. Have you ever had your life suddenly and utterly changed?"

The bartender, who had been an elementary school teacher in China until the time of the Cultural Revolution, when his house was smashed up with pickax handles, his head shaved, his wife beaten and raped in front of him, and both of them marched off to slave labor on a pig farm, smiled uncertainly, with carious teeth.

"Well, that's what happened to me," said George. He drank his eighth martini. "My life will never be the same. You see before you a broken man. I have no illusions anymore, and no ambitions, really. All I want to do is sell the inn, divorce my wife, and go to England. The newspapers are much better there."

"Order now, sir?" asked a Vietnamese woman in a rayon cheongsam.

"Yes. The entirety of your richly ecumenical menu, please, and extra fortune cookies. Tell me." George clutched her hand. "Have you ever had your life suddenly and utterly changed?"

"I escape Vietnam on small boat and we eat old people who die. I learn English. Now I am in computer school."

"Then you know what I mean!" said George excitedly. "It's very liberating, isn't it? It's a *fabulous* experience. When you realize that nothing fucking matters—when you hit that absolute apex, that shining pinnacle, of human intellectual potentia—you're free. Absolutely fucking free. You have become a member, as it were, of the Illuminati." George turned gravely to the bartender. "Another martini, you, there's a good fellow."

"No more! Too much drink! I call manager!"

"Look. There's a goddamned blizzard out there, and drunk or sober, I probably won't make it home alive anyway. You don't have any other customers, and I *promise* I won't sue you, even if I remember where I was. I intend, sir, to get good and fucking drunk, absolutely ripped to the tits, and tell my wife exactly what I think of her. I don't know what I think of her, but I'll think of something. And if you don't serve me, you bastard, I will never patronize this establishment again. Look at all this money."

"Okay one more."

"Give me a scorpion thing. No, wait. The thing that comes in the skull. That's what I want. The thing in the skull. Listen to me carefully. I don't want any fruit, ice, or parasols. I want all the liquor you've got, and I want it in a human skull."

"Only ceramic."

"I'm not particular."

George felt transcendent. The bar of the Luau Dragon was overlit and shabby, with a Polynesian cannibal decor overlying (with the irrational paradoxicality of genuine Naturalism? wondered George) murals depicting Italian scenes, including a catastrophic eruption of Vesuvius—probably the big one, as far as George could tell. The establishment had previously been a spaghetti house, called La Cattiva, and it was actually here that George had, the summer after he graduated from college, become engaged to Magdalene. He had done it, he realized bitterly now, for no other reason than that she had stunned him by performing unreciprocated oral sex at almost every opportunity. George thought it was love: in truth it was a yeast infection.

The bartender delivered the drink, which was about a quart of light rum, with a floater of ignited dark rum flickering like the light of reason behind the eyeholes of a trepanned ceramic skull. George blew out the fire of intellect and chugged the concoction through a straw. He had a twinge of halcyon reminiscence.

"Frankly I think it was because I wasn't circumcised,"

he said to the aged bartender, who waved his hands like a traffic policeman ordering a car to stop.

"No English."

"No, I'm not English, just well educated. And I have a slight speech impediment. You know, it's strange how much you get your cock sucked before you're married, and how little, afterwards. Finished! Give me another one."

"No more drink."

"The fuck you say," said George raffishly.

Chapter 27

Cállate Tu Pinche Hocico

Jesus Castro had lied to Magdalene, of course, about not wanting to harm Tim Picasso, but he had not decided to kill him until Magdalene independently mentioned arson and murder, which opened up a new set of circumstances that had to be considered. Mr. Castro's way of life was fraught with various perils, but not only that: one had to constantly seek creative solutions to stimulating problems. This is what *every* businessman says, of course, but in Jesus Castro's case it actually happened to be true. That the problems to which Jesus Castro had to respond intellectually were the product of other people's creativity (sometimes homicidal, usually larcenous) was something Mr. Castro appreciated. It was very much like a game of chess, in Mr. Castro's mind—though, like most people who use chess as a metaphor, he had only the vaguest idea of what the game was like. As Simone prepared again to flog him, he was coming around to see that in this situation he had an opportunity to not only respond appropriately, and in due proportion restore the status quo, but to respond brilliantly, and elevate his reputation. Simone shook the tangles out of the cat-o'-nine-tails. Jesus Castro, handcuffed to the bed, stared into the infinite with the mystical expression of the artist on the verge of a masterpiece.

He had not come up here to kill anybody, yet there was no reason why he shouldn't, and if he was going to kill one person, he might as well kill everybody. In most business situations, it was best to kill as many people as possible. It cut down considerably on expenses, witnesses, and the number of things that could go wrong. Murphy's Law was no joke when you were marched manacled—a perversely exciting thought: he visualized Simone in a bailiff's outfit—before a grand jury.

Jesus Castro cogitated. He bit his lips. Magdalene had given him the idea of burning down the inn, true. But then *Hamlet* had originally been a folk story. Jesus Castro had recently come up with an idea for an incendiary device which he had not yet field-tested. It was very simple, like all good art. Materials needed: a waxed-paper cup, some gasoline, an ordinary dinner candle. You put gasoline in the cup (not too much), stood the candle in it, put one or more of these devices some place where a fire might have started anyway—and lit the candle before you left. It was brilliant, and probably untraceable. You only used a *little* gasoline—you didn't splash accelerants all over the place like an asshole.

He knew exactly how to burn down the inn. That was easy. The other elements of the problem were, one, retrieving the money, and two, figuring out how to kill everybody. In this he would have the assistance of Mr. Cervantes, who, come to think of it, should have already arrived from Miami. Killing was no big deal. It was easy to kill people who did not expect to be killed. You could look to history for many examples. Mr. Castro calculated that he would be dealing with three people who did not expect to be killed, and one who would be reassured, over Chinese food, that he would not be. Mr. Castro, a charming man to begin with, intended to be very disarming at dinner.

His thoughts were interrupted by a gorgeously painful cigarette burn on his left buttock, the faint smell of burnt flesh, and then a savage lash of the knotted cat.

"You filthy maricón," said Simone. "Scumbag. You disgusting cabrón."

"No, please," said Mr. Castro unconvincingly.

Chapter 28

In Which the Escremento
Hits the Ventaglio

Tim knew nothing about Jesus Castro's sexual habits. Even if he had, it would have been unreasonable to assume that it was Mr. Castro being loudly flogged in the next room by a woman who had begun to scream at him in Spanish. Tim, openmouthed, stood riveted in the middle of his room. Chains clattered. The cat fell. "Me asqueas," said the woman smokily. Listening carefully, Tim conjugated, translated. You disgust me. Slash. A hoarse inarticulate cry. "Me asqueas." Slash. "Cabrón." Goat. Slash. The man seemed to mumble something, which cut off into a muffled scream.

"¡Cállate tu pinche hocico! Maricón. ¡Me asqueas!"

Shut your animal mouth.

Slash, slash, slash, slash, slash. There was an orgasmic sob, then silence. Chains clanked. The bed creaked. Tim, eyes wide, left his room and went quickly downstairs. In the parlor, he was pouring himself a scotch when Magdalene came in, holding a large photo album. She looked very archly at him, but at the same time it was plain that she had been crying. She looked terrible. Her hair was in disorder, her mascara had run, and she looked like a girl playing Hamlet in a boarding school production. She stared at the scotch Tim had poured.

"That's not your whiskey."

Tim supposed it wasn't. He wondered if he was supposed to pour it back into the bottle. Magdalene sat primly
down on the sofa, the photo album on her knees.

"But go ahead—drink it. Be my fucking guest. Of course,
you are my fucking guest. And why, really, should one
amenity object to the misappropriation of another?" Magdalene thought a minute. "That's perfect," she said, as if it
satisfied her immensely. "I'm an amenity."

Tim had once gone out with a woman named
Amenity. He thought about her instead of what Magdalene
had been saying, and then remembered what Magdalene had
been saying.

"Oh God, no! Not at all."

"Yes I am."

"No, certainly not. It was all just a mistake."

Magdalene did not move for a moment, then sat smartly
erect. "Fine. A mistake."

"Oh, come on."

"No, of course you're right. It was a mistake." She
snapped pages in the album. "These are photographs of
other mistakes. That's mainly what photographs are. You
look at them and you see yourself in the wrong places,
wearing the wrong clothes, with exactly the wrong people.
And here's a wedding picture. I wasn't just suddenly married to George, you know, out of nowhere."

"No, of course not."

"I mean, I must have married him on purpose. There
was obviously some reason. I'm looking at these pictures to
see if I can discover what it was. I was smoking a lot of pot at
the time, and I thought George was a poet. I hadn't read any
poetry. Would you like to look at my wedding pictures?"

"No, thank you."

Magdalene quizzed at him, head cocked, and then smiled with bright theatrical indifference. She leafed through the pages of the album. She looked very pleased with herself.

"Someone's here to see you," she said.

"I beg your pardon?" asked Tim.

"I didn't say anything," said Magdalene.

The doorbell rang. Magdalene looked significantly at Tim.

"There's the doorbell gone, as George says, God damn him. Do you want to answer the door?"

"It's not my inn."

"It isn't? I supposed it was, the way you've been helping yourself to everything. Oh, fuck the doorbell."

Magdalene threw the photo album across the room, shattering a dusty lamp in the shape of a diapered Indian mahout, and went to answer the door. Tim overheard the conversation.

"Chíngame. These fucking snow."

"How lovely. Another Hispanic."

Tim bolted through into the next room, where he stood uncertainly in the shadows by the derelict grand piano. On top of the piano was a photograph of George's parents. Mr. Hawthorne was a tiny scowling fat man, and Mrs. Hawthorne, beaming at the photographer, in front of the Admiral Benbow, looked exactly like George, but with breasts and goiter.

"I'm here to see a guy name Brian Wassermann."

"Exactly. I suppose you're Disraeli. The Sephardim are

everywhere. Mr. Wassermann's on the second floor, the second room along to your right. I believe he's handcuffed to his bed."

Tim peered down the hall. A young Cuban man, very sharply dressed, in a lime-colored ensemble and canary shoes, turned and thundered upstairs. Tim instantly recognized him. It was Mr. Cervantes, whom Tim had last seen lying by the pool at Jesus Castro's house, drinking rum and indifferently shooting pelicans with a silenced machine pistol. Oh shit, thought Tim. Running footsteps passed overhead, and there was a sharp pounding on a door.

"Boss! Boss!"

"What the fuck," said Jesus Castro. "Can' you let me relax?"

"La puta en la sala de entrada—"

"Can' I get laid? Whassa matta with you?"

"Ah. ¿La sadista?"

"Sí. Go downstairs. Pretty soon we have some Chinese. You see my friend, you don' let him go. I ain' talk to him yet. I be down little while. Tied up right now, ain' I, baby?"

"¡Cállate tu pinche hocico! Maricón. ¡Rebájate!"

Tim had no idea what to do. Footsteps passed overhead. He was not particularly a man of action, being an artist, and thus sedentary and paranoid, but in some district of his imagination he had always been swinging a sword, blowing off heads, saving the colors, boarding ships under fire. He suddenly dashed along the passage into the lobby, just as Mr. Cervantes's yellow shoes were descending the stairs, and he reached through the spokes of the banister and grabbed a skinny, lavender-socked ankle.

Mr. Cervantes, his leg arrested and the upper half of his body still moving forward, opened his mouth, wind-milled his arms in shock, but made no sound of any kind, except the inevitable sequence of thuds as he fell down the stairs. Tim raced around the end of the banister and kicked Mr. Cervantes smartly under the chin, which was enough to knock him out, even if his head hadn't smashed through one of the thick lower panes of the English tele-phone box.

Mr. Cervantes rolled on the floor. Tim leaped on him and searched him. Mr. Cervantes had no weapon except a switchblade, which, when clicked, turned out to be a comb. Tim tossed it aside. Mr. Cervantes had obviously flown commercial.

"Get me some rope," he whispered as Magdalene came up beside him.

Magdalene did nothing at first but smooth her hair. Then she said, with bright logic, "I'm going to tell Mr. Wassermann."

"No. No, you can't. These people are here to kill me."

Magdalene knew better. They were here to kill George and burn down the inn. That was what was important. Other considerations may have existed, but they were not, of course, Magdalene's concern.

"Mr. Wassermann wouldn't hurt a fly," she said. Then she thought about it. It didn't seem to make sense, of course, since he was going to give her an estimate for assas-sinating George, but things so seldom did make sense, and she started for the stairs.

Tim tackled her. Magdalene lay entirely passive, which

was largely the result of the Xanax she had been eating like peanuts for most of the day.

"I'm very, very serious. Mr. Wassermann isn't Mr. Wassermann. His name is Jesus."

"I beg your pardon?"

"Hay*sus*. His name is Jesus Castro, and he's a cocaine smuggler from Miami. He's come here to kill me."

"Then why haven't you left?"

"I didn't know he was here."

"Why would he want to kill you?" asked Magdalene.

"I stole a million and a half dollars from him."

"And where is this my fault?"

"What?"

"I asked if it was my fault," repeated Magdalene, and then looked at Tim, her lip trembling.

Tim completely lost his mind. "No, of course it isn't your fault. But it is your *problem*. If they kill me, they'll obviously kill you, and George, and Simone, because you've seen them here, and can identify them."

"Not necessarily," said Magdalene.

"What?"

"Look, Tim, I'm sorry, but at this juncture in my life I really need to put myself first, and I just can't think about other people. Nor do I want to imagine that my actions have consequences. I've never liked thinking that they do. It's just too complicated. And you don't love me, anyway."

"You're out of your trees."

"Well, why wouldn't I be? I've been terribly hurt."

"By me?"

"No, of course not. I don't care about you at all. It was

just sex. Frankly, at this phase in my life, I need not to need men."

"Magdalene, obviously there are things we can discuss later, but right now I have to tie up Mr. Cervantes. For God's sake, you don't want to tell the man upstairs. Trust me. I'll take care of everything."

"Will you really?" Magdalene hugged him and started kissing him all over the face and head. Tim extricated himself.

"Magdalene. Please just go and have a cup of tea or something."

"I love you."

"I have great affection for you, which may be love. It confuses me. But right now I have to tie up Mr. Cervantes, and I need some rope or something."

"I'll get some!" Magdalene was excited now.

"Thank you very much, Magdalene."

Before she came back with the duct tape and the clothesline, Tim was forced to hit Mr. Cervantes again, this time with the forty-pound registration ledger.

Chapter 29

Après George le Deluge

George made it home nearly without incident. He was
very drunk, the roads were unbelievably bad, the storm
was more violent than any he had ever seen or imagined,
and the visibility nil. But he took to driving like a man who
had finally learned the trick of a video game, and hurled
the Volvo confidently through exploding snowdrifts, front
yards, and over a section of a golf course.

The car spun out lordly on several occasions, causing
George to spill some rum, and to rear-end a Honda (it happened to be rented to Mr. Pilosi, who was staggering toward
the inn through a Hispanicized Jack London story) aban-
doned in a snowdrifted intersection. But it was quite obvious to George now that there was no problem he could not
solve. He had the secret of life. He didn't give a damn.
Drinking rum from the human skull, he motored on casu-
ally though the nor'easter, listening to AC/DC.

Four enormous bags of Chinese food were on the passenger seat, shifting, collapsing, reeking, and George occasionally reached out a hand to steady them. He finished
the skull of rum and pulled over in someone's yard, smash-
ing a plaster donkey, to refill the skull from the bottle he
had in the glove compartment. It had been some work getting the skull from the Luau Dragon. In fact there had been
a surreal altercation in the snow, in which tall George,
clutching the skull as well as four huge bags of food, had

found himself surrounded by what seemed to be *thousands* of small shouting Chinese persons, who made grabs for the skull but eventually went away.

The skull stared at George with empty eye sockets as he filled up again with rum, ignoring a man in a sou'wester pounding at his window. He drove on toward the inn. The coast road was problematic. There was no snow on it, but that was only because waves kept breaking over it, and great sections were beginning to be washed away. George was not aware that anything was out of order on Atlantic Road until suddenly the Volvo, which he had guided deftly around a policeman who waved a flashlight at him, was struck by a monstrous wave, full of boulders, telephone poles, and uprooted trees.

Two of the side windows blew in, the car blasting full of salt water, and though George turned the wheel with what he thought was intelligent deliberation, the car slewed in the other direction like a carnival whip, then rolled over violently three times. Much to George's surprise, he found himself to be still motoring along—not on the road, it was true, but through three feet of wreckage, foam, and sea-water in the yard of a destroyed summer home.

The Volvo was making clanking noises, one of the tires had blown out, and it was half full of water, but the bags of Chinese food had not ruptured, and George, although his eyeglasses were smashed, and dangling from one ear, still had his skull full of rum. He guided the Volvo carefully back onto the road, just in time for the car to be nearly flattened beneath a collapsing forty-foot breaker. This time the remaining windows blew out, because the roof was crushed, but George simply floored the gas pedal, downshifted, barely escaped being dragged off the road and into the sea, and was suddenly clanking and roaring uphill and away from the bad part of the coast road, the windshield gone, and one wiper, bent, a strand of kelp fluttering from it, still beating at the empty air.

"Fucking Volvo!" George cried in ecstasy. "No shit."

Blinded by the snow, but exhilarated and howling, George slammed the car through the three feet of water that had flooded the causeway, and roared uphill into the inn's driveway (thirty feet above sea level, the Admiral Benbow was not getting the worst of it—not yet) and instantly collided with Archy Lafata's Malibu. Archy toppled backward over the wall of the sunken rose garden, and smashed anoraked through the roof of the greenhouse, along with a quarter-ton of snow. George, oblivious, emptied the skull of rum, grabbed the disintegrating bags of Chinese food, and climbed like a tank commander through the Volvo's shattered sunroof. He slogged through the snowdrifts and flying spume toward the inn, the lights of which flickered and then went comprehensively out.

Lights Out

There were only two people in the world who knew that Jesus Castro was afraid of the dark. One was his mother, a saintly woman, whom he had brought over from Cuba with great reverence and at great expense, during the difficult period when he had been a pimp. The other was his older brother, Umberto, a perfect bastard who had been switching off lights and hurling Jesus Castro into dark places since he was a child. Still Umberto would do this, whenever he came over to the house. He would throw circuit breakers, unscrew lightbulbs, and pretend to be a monster, coming at Jesus Castro in a hooded blanket, one hand hooked into a horror-film claw. Even though Jesus Castro knew rationally that it was only Umberto, he still, even at the age of thirty-five, had a fifty-percent chance of wetting his pants when the lights went out and Umberto started chuckling.

So naturally, when the lights went out at the Admiral Benbow, Jesus Castro immediately thought of Umberto, whose very name filled him with dread. He stopped breathing. His scalp prickled. The darkness was intense. Jesus Castro became incapable of rational thought. *Umberto had found him and was in the hotel.* He started shouting.

"Light a match! I can' see nothing. Light a fucking match!"

Simone held up her butane lighter. It was a terrifying

little guttering flame, which could not improve, and would only go out. Jesus Castro searched the room spastically for anything that would light, burn. Whining, he clicked the light switches.

"What's wrong with you?" asked Simone.

"Nothing. You hear some body?"

"No."

Just then there was a slow, dreadful knock on the door. Jesus Castro had an impulse to hide under the bed, but he remembered he was an adult. He also remembered that he had firearms, quite a lot of them, and he grabbed his Uzi, just as Simone's lighter went out. If the safety had not been on, Jesus Castro would have shot the hell out of Norman's Woe.

"Light that fucking thing!"

"It's lit, actually," said George's cheerful voice from the other side of the door. Fearfully, in the light of the relit butane lighter, Jesus Castro jerked open the door. George, soaking wet, stood there listing hospitably, and holding up an oil lamp which lit him like a Rembrandt portrait.

"Jesus Christ," said Jesus Castro. "You scare the shit outa me. Whassa matta? Lights go out?"

"The storm, I'm afraid," said George ethereally.

"Don' talk to me that voice."

"No electricity," said George. "Societal breakdown has started. And do you know what?"

"You tell me," said Jesus Castro.

"I don't give a damn."

"No good to have no power and lights and shit," said Jesus Castro.

George dug in his pocket and pulled out a damp, bent

cigarette. "Personally, Mr. Wassermann, I always wanted to be an eighteenth-century man. Syphilis and lack of public sanitation aside, I think I would have been most happy as a contemporary of Dr. Swift." George lit his cigarette off the oil lamp.

"I don' know what you talk aboud."

George leaned forward. "I don't give a shit." He turned to Simone. "Simone? I'd like to talk to you about something personal later on, if it's all right."

"Sure," said Simone.

"Your Chinese food is downstairs, Mr. Wassermann. My future ex-wife is setting the table as we speak—or rather, as I speak, and you stand there looking like a fucking idiot."

Jesus Castro was too stunned to respond. George slammed the door, and left the room in darkness, which caused Jesus Castro to urinate—not profusely, but enough to matter.

"He don' know who I am, talk to me that way. You know who I am?"

"Yeah, you're a scumbag," said Simone, and pulled his hair.

Chapter 31

Have Some Nice Chinese

George left the oil lamp on the hall table and, lighting a taper from its flame with drunken absorption, went along to his room, where, feeling festive for some reason, he changed his wet clothes for evening dress, complete with cummerbund. On the wall above the fireplace was a Navy cutlass, and he stuck that in his cummerbund, then put on his tasseled mortarboard before going back downstairs.

The lights had gone off all over Tyburn, and one of the electric lights that was extinguished with the rest happened to be the single bulb in the workshed on the jetty, where a half-thawed Mr. Briscoe lay sprawled dreamily by the propane heater. When Tim had opened the door of the shed, with the bound, gagged, and unconscious Mr. Cervantes on his shoulder, it was at that exact moment that the light went out, preventing him from seeing Mr. Briscoe. So Tim had gone about his business and deposited Mr. Cervantes on what he supposed was the floor.

It struck Tim as very odd that the workshed seemed to be heated (to what had to be well over a hundred degrees), but there were many unusual things in life, and he hadn't time for all of them. At least Mr. Cervantes, whose head had fallen invisibly onto Mr. Briscoe's survival-suited lap, would not freeze to death. Tim had already rejected the idea of tossing Mr. Cervantes into the cove, and he realized that the shed's being heated preserved him further from the possibility of being a murderer. He went back up to the inn fairly cheerfully, enjoying things.

Magdalene was setting plates on the big dining room table when George entered, in evening dress, cutlass, and mortarboard. George sat down and started shoveling moo shoo pork into a flaccid palmed pancake. Magdalene noted that George was extremely drunk.

"The car's wrecked," he said.

"Good."

"I nearly got killed."

"Excellent."

George ate moo shoo for a while.

"Mr. Wassermann has a submachine gun," he said.

"I'm not surprised," said Magdalene. "He's really named Jesus, he's from Miami, and he's come here to kill Tim. He'll probably kill us, too."

"Oh, the *fuck* he will," said George. He slammed his cutlass on the table, piratically, and drank some soy sauce from a plastic container.

"I don't know why I'm telling you anything, George. I don't know why I'm talking to you. You're drunk."

"Fuck you," said George.

"George!" Magdalene was genuinely shocked. "What did you say to me?"

"I said, 'Fuck you.' Is there any sauce for this stuff?" George lunged for the lazy Susan. Jesus Castro peered shakily into the dining room. He was relieved by the level and quality of the light—in a different way from how he was relieved by the darkness—for the old room was full of burning candles.

"What the fuck you got on your head?" he asked George.

"A thinking cap," said George. "The dazzling halo of Western Civilization is what I've got on my head."

"Hey. Who you talk to?"

"I'm talking to you. Now, why don't you sit down and eat some Chinese food before I kill you."

"George?" said Magdalene.

"No one appreciates me. I had to wrestle all these Chinamen in the parking lot."

"He's been drinking," said Magdalene, with ludicrous suburban discretion.

"From a human skull," said George. "Have you ever drunk from a human skull, Mr. Whoever You Are?"

"George!"

"I bet he hasn't."

Jesus Castro didn't know quite what to do. No one had ever even *thought* about talking to him like this—he had once shot a man in the pelvis for patting his bichon frise— but the lights had gone out, he had pissed himself, and had there been an analyst available, he might have admitted that hurting or killing people who offended him was a form of aggressive denial of the fact that he really *was* just a scumbag from Florida. A scumbag from Florida, furthermore, who was afraid of the dark, his elder brother, palmetto bugs, and homosexuality, in just about that order. On top of everything else, "scumbag" was a word frequently used of Mr. Castro while he was under the lash, and it had confusing sexual connotations. He sat down humbly at the table.

"We will now say grace," said George. "Jesus having joined us. Dearly beloved—your tropical eminence—

honored guests. We are gathered here to celebrate the end of the short, unhappy marriage of George and Magdalene Hawthorne."

"Have some rice." Magdalene passed it to Jesus.

"Excuse me," said George, "but would you favor me with the fucking mustard?"

"Look, guy, I know you drunk, but you don' talk like that front of no lady," said Jesus Castro.

George begged to differ. "I have quarreled with my country, sir, and a man who has quarreled with his country is under no obligation to his wife. Have an egg roll, Savior," said George.

An egg roll bounced off Jesus Castro's head. He then very deliberately turned to Magdalene.

"Look, lady, I see why you ask me what you do, and I thing aboud, but now, between you and me, I jus' wan' to finis' my business and go home to Miami. These guy is no my problem."

George momentarily ceased to be anyone's problem, because he had passed out cold at the table, with his face in a plate of chow yoke.

"You wan' me to kill him now, some time?"

"No," said Magdalene quickly. "I've taken care of it." She looked at George with his face in his plate. "I poisoned him."

"Okay. These guy come here for me. Where he go now today some time?"

"I don't know," said Magdalene. "He went . . . out."

"Out?"

"Yes. He went out to get some cigarettes."

"Cigarette? He don' smoke no cigarette. What the fuck

you say to me. I get all this nice Chinese. I tip good. I don'
kill this guy hits me on the head with fucking egg roll. I don'
cause no problem, but you tell me a guy go get cigarette
when I know he don' smoke cigarette. Beside, look the fuck
snow."

"I meant—your other friend. The one you don't want to
hurt."

"I don' wanna hurt no one," said Jesus Castro emphat-
ically. He was the picture of sincerity. "I don't wanna hurt
you, and between you and me, I wasn' even gonna kill this
asshole even if you give the money to me. That is how serious I happen to be about be nice guy some time. So what
aboud."

Tim, who had emerged quietly from the gloom, cracked
Mr. Castro sharply on the back of the head with his pistol.
For a moment, although there was a sound like a melon
being hit with a baseball bat, the blow had no effect. Jesus
Castro merely sat as he was, with exactly the same sincerely
interrogative expression, looking worldly, self-aware, and
businesslike. But then his eyes rolled white, he dropped
the breaded shrimp he had been gesturing with, and pitched
sideways out of his chair, as Tim watched interestedly, and
as Magdalene realized that she was, of all things, more
aroused than she'd ever been in her life.

The Singular Adventures
of Mr. Cervantes in the Tool Shed

Mr. Briscoe awoke from a dream of a ballet of cherubs dancing around a large red party shoe with a spiked heel—a vision of such transcendent clarity, integrity, and glory that when it ended he woke with a sob. He had no idea where he was. It was pitch-dark, wherever it was, he was soaked with sweat, he had a broken arm, and he was holding . . . the one good thing . . . the red shoe from his toolbox. The bad thing was that there seemed to be some sort of animal on his lap.

Mr. Briscoe prodded fearfully at whatever it was, and it moved slightly. Then, just as he was about to scream, the single lightbulb flickered on in the room, and he saw that what was on his lap was not an animal, but a young man's head, with a pair of terrified brown eyes that looked up at him beseechingly from a face whose lower half was covered with duct tape.

Mr. Briscoe had always been very particular about not being a homosexual, but from time to time he had considered what kind of boys he'd go for if he was (which he wasn't). And Mr. Cervantes, whether Mr. Briscoe was or wasn't, was exactly it.

"I'll be goddamned," said Mr. Briscoe. "I might give her a whirl if my arm wasn't broke."

He sat up slightly and painfully and looked very closely at Mr. Cervantes.

"I expect you're a faggot," said Mr. Briscoe.

Mr. Cervantes's eyes widened. He shook his head.

"Yep. Look at them yellow shoes. How can you lie there with them yellow shoes and tell me you ain't a faggot. Do I look like I was born yesterday?"

Mr. Briscoe, who actually had pre-gangrenous patches of frostbite on his face, and even with medical attention would have lost his nose, did not look at all as if he had been born at any time within the last hundred fifty years, much less yesterday. He had lost his partial upper plate while screaming for help, his hair was in salt-crusted corkscrews, and he had never been a handsome character anyway. He glared lasciviously at Mr. Cervantes, his crooked bottom teeth protruding beyond his sucked-in upper lip.

"I just want to wear this red shoe," said Mr. Briscoe, holding it up so Mr. Cervantes could see it. "It don't mean nothing dirty."

It should be mentioned that Mr. Briscoe was also deaf in one ear, and basically couldn't hear out of the other. He was not actually saying anything, so much as shouting. Mr. Cervantes started to cry.

"I said I'd give it a whirl if I come through alive," said Mr. Briscoe, philosophically, "and broke arm or no, I reckon I owe a few things to merciful Almighty God, the Baker-man of my salvation, who, come to think on it, probably sent me this sign of His continuing affection. Shall the thing made say to Him who made it, why hast Thou made me thus?"

Mr. Cervantes rolled his head off Mr. Briscoe's lap and tried to jackknife away from him. Mr. Briscoe grasped the edge of his workbench, and levered himself upright into the blast-furnace heat of the shed. He put down the red pump and admired it. It was a corker of a shoe. Mr. Briscoe was distracted by the climate.

"Goddam heat's way up in the stratosphere." Thriftily he switched off the heater. "I don't expect the subject comes up in the circles you move in, boy, but a tank of propane don't cost peanuts anymore, and neither do peanuts for that matter. I won't buy peanuts. I won't give them the satisfaction. Besides, I can get all the peanuts I want down the Elks. That's where I get my peanuts, when I got a yen for peanuts. Down the Elks."

Mr. Cervantes, who was still crying, thought Mr. Briscoe was saying "penis."

"Yeah. Down the Elks is where I go when I got a cravin' for peanuts. I got no taste for that other stuff they got there, them snack bags. My word, boy, it's hot as the hinges of hell. I don't expect it was you that turned her on up, but just so you don't in the future. You want me to take that tape off your face, or you like her like that?"

Mr. Cervantes did not respond, and after a minute Mr. Briscoe forgot he had asked a question. He was struggling laboriously out of the salt-crusted survival suit.

"This is a good piece of equipment," said Mr. Briscoe. "Like to meet the man that invented it, buy him a drink, shake his hand. This one here's made over in Norway, get me, and don't get me wrong, them Swedes is good people, but I'll bet you a barrel of apples to your five cents that the man that *designed* this contraption was an American. Country's gone straight to shit, son. Painful to see. Right goddam painful. I know what the problem is with the country these days, and I'm going to lay it all out for you, boy, but before I go on, I'm going to make a remark preparative to my subject. I'm a bigot. I was born and raised a bigot. Both my mother and father were bigots. I listened for a while to what they have to say on the TV about the subject of bigotry, and then one day I couldn't stand it anymore. Shot the TV right off the kitchen counter. Give it both barrels, one after the other, about three in the mornin'. Ten-gauge, boy. That's two bigger than a twelve-gauge. The neighbors come over hopin' I shot myself. They want to make a driveway where my house is. But that's got nothing to do with the price of onions, boy. My point is that I finally realized that there ain't nothing wrong, on the evidence, with being a bigot.

"I imagine you're an Italian. Well, I don't even like I-talians yet. Goddam spaghetti-benders on the one hand, running questionable trucking businesses, and you got the Polacks on the other hand. Let me tell you something, son. Between you and me, I never met a Polack with enough brains to fry eggs. Son, I have questioned my bigotry. I don't know if you understand. I have questioned it and still come up a bigot. Your goddam Irish are a bunch of goddam drunks. I don't mind taking a snort myself, from time to time, but there's a difference between the way a white man drinks and the way an Irishman drinks."

Mr. Briscoe unbuckled his belt.

"You know what a stereotype is, boy?"

Mr. Cervantes, with wide eyes, shook his head.

"A stereotype," said Mr. Briscoe, coiling his belt neatly, "is something obvious, widely observed, absolutely correct, and totally unacceptable. That's what a stereotype is, boy. It's the goddam *truth*."

Mr. Briscoe stepped hideously out of his long johns.

"Country's going to hell in a handbasket because you can't say anything true! Everyone wants bullshit, bullshit, and more bullshit. Well, I don't want no more bullshit. I don't like wops, micks, kikes, French Canadians, niggers, spics, women, retards, cripples, faggots, Mormons, or Hindu dot-headed sons of bitches. What I like is myself, and other men of original stock who work with their goddam hands, believe in God, know how to make whiskey, bricks, or a windmill, can write a coherent letter, and don't say much unless severely agitated, *which I am*."

Mr. Briscoe, hideously nude, paused dramatically.

"And what I'm gonna do now, boy, is tear myself off a piece of ass, and you're it."

Chapter 33

Art for the Masses

Tim stood horripilated by what he had done. Knocking out and tying up Mr. Cervantes was one thing, but pistol-whipping Jesus Castro was quite another. He ran to the lobby and looked out the front door. The driveway was full of wrecked and buried cars. No lights whatsoever were visible on the mainland, except for some orange emergency flashers perhaps two miles away along the coast, and hardly even visible. Archy Lafata was sitting anoraked in his idling car, but Tim wasn't aware of this because the car was a perfect drumlin of snow, like a barrow grave with exhaust coming out of it. Tim pushed the door shut against the wind, and went back into the dining room with duct tape fresh from the Cervantes job and a roll of speaker wire.

"I may have to kill these two guys, Magdalene. Do you have any problem with that?"

"No," said Magdalene.

"I mean, if I don't kill them, they'll keep coming after me, and I don't see how I'd get anything done."

"You seem to be very good at being a criminal."

"I'm good at everything," said Tim. "It's my tragedy."

"You can't be good at *everything*."

"The true artist is good at everything he touches. Unless you're a universal artist, you're not an artist at all. There are a few people I'd like to say that to, while I smash their heads into the pavement."

"Maybe you should calm down."

"The point is, if you're not a genius, *don't bother*."

"That's what I tell George."

"I *know* I shouldn't have stolen money from a drug smuggler, I know I should have tried something else, but I like nice things, and couldn't see how else to get my start. I have lots of connections, but nearly all of them are terrified of me. Sometimes I sit up at night wishing that I was mediocre."

Tim bent to wildly wrap duct tape around Jesus Castro's head. It tore off clumps of his hair. "Now I'm good at being a criminal. I'm going to lose interest in it. You watch. It's a pattern."

"You're being pretty extreme," said Magdalene politely.

"Don't listen to her," said George weakly, his face still planted in chow yoke. "She kills artists with her bourgeois pragmatism. That sounds like a space weapon. It isn't. It's merely the way she gets up in the morning. I'm warning you! She has no imagination at all."

"Shut up, George," said Magdalene. "I honestly don't know how you can expect people to take you seriously when"—she tried to think of what to say—"when—you have a penis the size of a cocktail shrimp."

"The hell I do!" George roared, and reeled upright. His face was covered in gravy, and bits of mushroom and beef fell off his face as he staggered about in half-controlled circles, digging in the front of his trousers.

"Don't," said Tim.

"She's always saying things like that," said George.

"She thinks I won't show anybody. Look at this. Does this look like a cocktail shrimp?"

"Jesus," said Tim. "What have you been telling him?"

"Well, okay, it's not all that small, but he's terrible in bed," said Magdalene, defensively. "And even if he wasn't I'd say so, because I can."

"My God, what if I went around saying you had an enormous vagina, as if it explained your behavior." George headed for the drinks. "Oceans of ink have been spilled on the subject of Hemingway's penis, but does anyone ever say, 'Yeah, but what about Barbara Cartload's baggy old cunt?'"

"George!"

"Gertrude Stein," roared George, "had a cavernous twat and furthermore was one."

"You're drunk!" shouted Magdalene.

"Of course I'm drunk, you colossal . . . mitten."

Magdalene looked at Tim.

"It's Chaucerian."

"What's it mean?

"'Cunt.'"

"Oh, nice language, George."

"Do you know that I was actually considering being flagellated? She," said George, pointing at Magdalene with the cutlass (Tim grappled it away), "made me feel that bad. Why are you tying up Mr. Wassermann?"

"So he won't kill us all," said Tim, putting the cutlass on the mantel. "It's difficult to explain."

"Don't bother," said George. "I don't care." And he tottered off to see Simone—but then something in the reptile part of his innkeeper's brain remembered Professor Eggman, and he staggered genially toward the billiards room to see about the Fiction People.

"He's not all that bad in bed, either," Magdalene said peevishly to Tim. "I just say that he is, because he has no way to tell if I'm lying."

"He seems to be in some ways completely changed," said Tim.

Just then there was a pounding at the front door, and Tim went to answer it. A short brutish man with a pointed bald head entered and removed his anorak. Tim aimed the pistol at the back of his head and cocked it, but then hid it when the man turned around.

"You must be a writer," said Tim.

"Oh ya," said Archy Lafata cleverly. "My name is *John Wong.*"

Tim decided shrewdly to say nothing.

"Anyway, I took some time off from bangin' away at my writin' and so forth, because there's a guy over here dressed as a pirate I need to talk to."

"Okay."

"He owes me a thousand bucks for drinks. And incidentally, you people owe me some money, too. Some guy hit me with a car in your driveway and I fell through a glass sunlight and got this thing stuck in my ass."

He held up a gardening claw.

"Kill him," said Magdalene.

George made his way decorously toward the billiards room, peering out the gallery windows at the terrace. It looked to him as if the snow had become motile out there, and was not only moving but carrying with it items of furniture, deck chairs and Cinzano umbrellas and so forth. It was actually not *snow* George was looking at, but sea foam, with green seawater beneath it—fifteen feet higher than it should have been—but George had no idea about that. Waves were breaking on the balustrade of the terrace itself, with huge concussions that caused spray to shoot fifty feet into the air. The fall of the spray on the roof of the inn sounded like biblical deluges of cinder blocks and bricks and cars. But George simply went along making sure the doors and windows were locked, just as he did every evening after dinner. When he entered the small glassed sunporch he not only found himself standing in four inches of water, but discovered a desiccated young man in a pirate costume. Mr. Glowery had managed to break a window and open the French door, and was now shivering violently on a Victorian daybed, trying to cover himself with a few louvered blinds and a piece of carpet. The sunporch was filling rapidly with snow, which whirled through the broken window. George stared at Mr. Glowery: a pirate! Probably been a shipwreck, like in the book. Now George had something to do.

"Can I help you?" George asked the pirate.

Mr. Glowery was staring as well, at a very drunk man in a tasseled mortarboard.

"I don't think so," said Mr. Glowery.

George took a swig of his cocktail and sat down and handed it to Mr. Glowery, who drank the rest of it. Mr. Glowery looked about as good as Mr. Briscoe. His eyes were feverish and visionary. George sat down on the edge of the daybed and straightened his dickey and tie.

"Were you shipwrecked, then?" asked George.

"I am guilty of hubris," said Mr. Glowery in a weird, thin voice. "I will be done to death."

"Right. Well, there's some Chinese food in the dining room, Admiral. Just go along that way, and up the stairs to the main wing. Go two doors along and take a right. In the hubris department, as far as that goes, my wife and a guy who can't figure out what art form is large enough for him have got Jesus tied up on the floor."

"I don't think I could handle that at the moment," said Mr. Glowery.

"Well, there's also the literary workshop in the billiards room. There's no hubris *there*."

"Yes," said Mr. Glowery. "Thank you." He tried to stand. George tried to help him and managed only to rip his parrot off. George looked at the parrot. Its beak was parted in a silent scream. It had only one eye. He handed the parrot back to Mr. Glowery, and grappled him to his feet. It proving that Mr. Glowery could not stand independently, George, hospitably, crammed him into a wicker bath chair and dragged him along the corridor toward the billiards room.

Chapter 34

Clenched, Turgid

W hat we want in short fiction," Professor Eggman was saying, "American short fiction, is something I like to call the *'poignant almost.'* Can anyone tell me what that might be?"

No one said anything. Joel Josh O'Connor was frozen over his notepad, terrified of being called on.

"Saraswati?"

Professor Eggman came promptly to the conclusion that Saraswati, in her Senegalese head-wrap, in particular had no idea what he was talking about.

"Well, Saraswati, let us criticize your story in terms of—through the *lens* of—the *poignant almost.* Dressed in Third World garments and menstruating, you go to the seashore during a full moon and, by moonlight, ritualistically bury a pumpkin which you've . . . you've . . . cut open . . . and filled with various sorts of crap . . . and fluids—"

"My *character* buries a pumpkin," said Saraswati severely.

"—in hopes of attracting a sub-Saharan paramour, with whom you will produce illegitimate mixed-race and magically real children that in your view the world requires to achieve perfection."

"Right."

"Now, if you stop the story *immediately after* the pumpkin is buried, *and before there is any result*, *then* you have a literary short story: fraught and poignant, dense with magic. Get out before anything happens. Then by God you're paring your fingernails."

"'Paring your fingernails'?" asked Saraswati.

"Like Joyce."

No one said anything.

"Who's Joyce?" asked Saraswati.

"James. Irishman. The artist is remote, paring his fingernails."

"What's that got to do with anything?"

"Well, look. If you carry the story past that natural closure (the pumpkin burying and the hoping), and actually *do* attract a lover and produce children, what you have isn't literary short fiction, Saraswati, but a concluded fairy tale. Which is literature only if you're a South American."

"That's judgmental."

"As is the world, my dear Saraswati."

"And negative."

"Necessarily," said Professor Eggman.

"And racist."

Even Professor Eggman had had enough.

"Look, young lady, you're white, you're wearing Third World garments, and your hobby is black people. Your story is about procuring an African man through an act of magic, against his will, for your own supposedly Utopian purposes. *It's morally equivalent to slavery and rape.*"

"But he would love me—"

George dragged Mr. Glowery's bath chair into the circle

of chairs. "I found a pirate on the porch," he announced drunkenly.

"Ah, Mr. Negro has joined us," said Professor Menelaus Eggman. "There's a man for the Poignant Almost."

Everyone stared at Mr. Glowery. His pirate costume was shredded and he was gripping his parrot like a scepter of office.

"Non serviam," he said.

Saraswati was always emboldened by seeing another person in obscure transcultural garb and always made a particular point of observing the customs of other cultures.

"Non serviam," she said to Mr. Glowery, and made a pranam.

Chapter 35

Mr. Briscoe's Second Thoughts,

Such As They Are

Homosexuality was not all that it was cracked up to be, in Mr. Briscoe's opinion. As he hobbled up to the hotel through the howling snowstorm, his broken arm in a sling, his right foot in the red high-heeled shoe, he had certain regrets about the whole experience, but absolutely no guilt. Mr. Briscoe genuinely intended, at the first opportunity, to tell the guys down the Elks. Damn the reaction! Mr. Briscoe bet himself anyway that there were more homos down the Elks than you might think.

He got to the front door of the inn, kicked it open, and staggered in and yelled out a hello. Nobody answered so Mr. Briscoe went for the whiskey in the parlor, clumping along in his red pump. The electric lights flickered and went out again. Mr. Briscoe paused in the darkness, and then went on, seeing candlelight burning dimly ahead in the dining room.

Jesus Castro had just come to full consciousness on the dining room floor when the lights went out again. He saw a figure in the darkness, limping, hunched, and dragging one foot, approaching him at a slow and dreadful pace. Umberto. Jesus Castro whined pitifully. Umberto came closer, one hand a claw, wearing a lumberjack cap with ear-flaps. Mr. Castro lost his reason.

Mr. Briscoe saw Mr. Castro lying on the floor, and went

closer, thinking, Damn if it isn't another one of them tied-up homosexuals. He went very close to Mr. Castro and peered down at him, his face frostbitten, upper plate missing, lower teeth protruding prognathously. He prodded Mr. Castro with his foot. Jesus Castro was trying to keep his eyes shut, and trying even harder not to wet himself, but finally he had to look. He wet himself again.

"Evenin'," said Mr. Briscoe, limping on into the candlelit parlor—and damn if what he saw right off the bat wasn't some youngster on the floor in front of the fireplace, going at it like the heavy hammers of hell with Mrs. Hawthorne. Mr. Briscoe wasn't even noticed as he went for the whiskey. At the drinks table, Mr. Briscoe poured himself a tumbler full of Crown Royal and drank it like ice water in the Sahara, and then poured another, which he was drinking with more moderation, less ecstatic snuffling, but equally intense satisfaction, when Mrs. Hawthorne started making noises of a character that Mr. Briscoe, a virgin (discounting Mr. Cervantes), found highly interesting. He had never heard such a thing in his life. He limped over and had a look.

Magdalene, eyes screwed shut, was repeating, mantra-like, something that struck Mr. Briscoe as being highly rhetorical.

"Be damned if he ain't doing that already," said Mr. Briscoe loudly.

Magdalene screamed at the sight of Mr. Briscoe, and had an orgasm simultaneously, which caused her expressions, in Mr. Briscoe's opinion, to be right contradictory. Tim looked around, haggard and alarmed.

"Howdy," said Mr. Briscoe. "Don't mind me. I'm just

having a snort of this whiskey before I hit the hay. Interestin' day, Mrs. Hawthorne. The hand of God has been everywhere."

"Mr. Briscoe. Your face—"

"I come out of the water alive, according to the plan of Providence, and I ain't objecting, either to that or the homo God left me down the shed. Shall the thing formed say to Him that formed it, why hast Thou made me thus? Nice set of tits there, Mrs. Hawthorne, if I do say so myself. The nakedness of woman is the work of God."

"Tim, this is Mr. Briscoe."

"How do you do, sir?"

"Can't complain," said Mr. Briscoe.

He refilled his glass.

"But Mr. Briscoe, sir, what's wrong with your face?"

"Bit banged up, I guess," said Mr. Briscoe, "and this arm's broke, and my boat sunk, but I come out of the water all right, I got my red shoe, and God sent me a tied-up homo, so I had myself a whirl. There's another one over there in the dinin' room, but I'm still tired out from the first one."

"Mr. Briscoe," said Magdalene, seizing an afghan, "you need an ambulance."

"The hell I do. I been in an ambulance."

"Mr. Briscoe—"

"Them sons of bitches charge insurance prices and I ain't got insurance. I won't give them the satisfaction. I been to the hospital once, for my appendix. Ate goddam Jell-O and lay there for two days without my cigarettes. Between you and me I'd rather die in the gutter. I coulda took the appendix out myself if I had a book."

Mr. Briscoe finished his fourth gigantic whiskey.

"Now I'm gonna go get me some shut-eye. Good to see you're gettin' some, Mrs. Hawthorne. I had my worries."

With that Mr. Briscoe limped off toward the stairs.

"He's wearing a woman's red shoe," said Tim quietly.

"No he was not."

"He was."

Chapter 36

Some Very Disastrous Events
Affecting the Billiards Room

A wave struck the hotel and the workshoppers screamed. George was making a racket behind the bar, making a drink for Archy Lafata, Professor Eggman, who held a buckled sheaf of papers, had broken out in a mild sweat trying to say that art was about *modest continual effort* (it kept coming out of him that art was about offhand and random "anti-masterpieces," which was no help to anybody— Professor Eggman had no idea in a million years what an "anti-masterpiece" might be, unless it was a piece of shit, and he didn't think that this was what his insanity intended). He was in no mood to listen to George cracking ice with a hammer and dropping things and chuckling drunkenly while he (Professor Eggman) was having quite enough trouble convincing his class that they hadn't been cheated. In desperation he turned to Mr. Glowery.

"Mr. Glowery, perhaps you could explain to the class—such as it is—what it's like being a professional writer in New York."

Mr. Glowery, his face frozen as if he were a Parkinson's victim, sat sideways in his chair, gripping his parrot. He was staring obliquely at Saraswati, his eyes bulging as if he were tripping and she were slowly turning into a monster, or his mother—essentially the same thing in some lighting.

"What it's like—doing . . . oh, I don't know, *writing*. What's it like writing a review?"

"Kill enemy," said Mr. Glowery. "Take money and women."

"Yes, but on a day-to-day basis."

Mr. Glowery, still staring at Saraswati, said nothing further. He raised his parrot slightly.

"*Right*," said Professor Eggman to the seminar in general. "Well, there you have it."

Archy Lafata, who had been watching the proceedings, at least insofar as they failed to proceed, suddenly got to his feet and cleared his throat.

"If none of youse guys are going to share, I'm going to stand up." He cleared his throat again. "My name's Archy, and I'm an alcoholic."

"Hello, Archy!" everyone said.

At that moment the windows of the billiards room blasted intriguingly white-with-foam, and then turned a solid dark green. Then they—and the wall they were set in—imploded. Mr. Glowery shrieked and, still sitting in his armchair, surfed off in a litter of firewood and old *New Yorkers*, shrieking, "He's killing us for sport!" The billiard table, collecting Archy Lafata as a passenger, slammed through the far wall and tumbled out onto the lawn. The chandelier streamed sideward and broke away, tearing the ceiling down with it, and landing on Saraswati. The wave retired, dragging with it Saraswati's corpse (which had become entangled with the noncorpse of the philosophical-looking Joel Josh O'Connor) and all of the furniture.

George found himself waist-deep in water, still holding his cocktail and preparing to make a remark about evacuation, when the second wave hit. The upper part of the wave smashed in the second-story windows, filled the attic with rocks, and knocked off one of the chimneys and part of a Victorian turret. Professor Menelaus Eggman, clutching a corner of the bar, was killed instantly by a shard of rusted plate from a sunken ship from the early days of ironclads.

George was blasted off his feet by a third sea, washed through the French doors, which had been holding back fifty thousand gallons of water, and sent surfing all the way into the kitchen, where he stood up vaguely, and closed the door that led to the billiards room. Another wave detonated against the house, shoving the wing in which George stood a full three feet off its foundation. Everything fell off the shelves in the kitchen. The door to the hall popped open again, and George closed it rather sensibly.

"My God," said Tim. He had come falling down the kitchen stairs. Water, filled with wreckage—a radio, a portrait of George's mother—was pouring into the kitchen from the upstairs hallway.

"I just realized something," said George. "I have a Ph.D. in English."

"George—"

"I'm not dead in the . . . water. Yet."

The door popped open yet again, and the headless corpse of Professor Menelaus Eggman floated into the kitchen and then was retracted by the backwash of the wave into the boiling sea.

"I rather fancy," said George, "that he isn't the Negro Bakerman now. Anyway, this is what I was thinking. I can go teach somewhere awful in New York City. I'll have a small life. A dingy apartment. A cat," he added significantly. "A cat. They hunt roaches, you know. Then in the fullness of time I'll commit suicide by sticking my head in the oven. Wifeless. Childless. Meaningless, unpublished, drunken, and old. I could just kill myself now, but I would always wonder if things might have gotten even worse."

"George. The entire building is coming apart. *Where's the fucking Fiction Workshop?*"

"Well, I don't think any of them were any good."

"That's irrelevant."

"Is it? In the larger sense?"

"I don't know."

"Well, two of them were swept out to sea in what they call the final embrace, and our particular guest Professor Menelaus Eggman was killed instantly by what looked to the layman to be a fragment of the *Andrea Doria*."

Tim peered openmouthed down the dark hallway. Water was swirling below the stairs that led down to the billiards room. A sofa was being dragged toward the boiling spectral sea beyond the smashed scrim of New England architecture. Tim seized George's flashlight and ran to the front of the hotel. When he managed to get the door open, he saw that a portion of a porch, or something very like a porch, with a piece of roof attached to it, and a stuffed owl attached to the roof, was doing thirty knots over the bottom as it crossed the driveway, slamming into Jesus Castro's car. Tim waded out into the front yard, up to his waist in foam, and was knocked down by a green sea which came roaring over Mr. Castro's Mercedes, containing Mr. Glowery, who grappled briefly with Tim in a rubbery way, shrieking "Serviam!" and then was dragged off the headland in a carnival of wreckage. Tim, dodging a shutter that spun off the hotel and nearly decapitated him, ran back to the hotel's granite front porch. He shone a light toward land. The causeway was covered by water or destroyed. The inn was cut off. Tim ran palely back inside.

"Water," said Tim. "We're cut off. The seaward wing's destroyed. The main house seems intact."

"Since 1801," said George, and belched.

"Look," said Tim. "This may have been fortunate."

"In what way?"

"How would you like three-quarters of a million dollars?"

Señor Cervantes

In the shed, Mr. Cervantes was smoking a cigarette and thinking serious thoughts. He had never been anywhere but south Florida, and the cultural and climatological shock—and now the sexual shock—had rendered him completely passive. His plane had circled Logan Airport for hours, then had landed in a blizzard. Two college girls had laughed at his clothes in the baggage area. He had gotten lost in the rented car. Upon arriving at the hotel, nearly in tears, he had suddenly blacked out in the middle of walking down some stairs, and then woke up in an inexplicable location, possibly an unadvertised sort of afterlife, where, as a further matter of metaphysical confusion, he had been slowly raped by what appeared to be a monster.

He had taken one terrified look out of the shed, after the monster had limped out, and saw nothing but a nightmare world of snow, and waves exploding over a collapsing breakwater at the end of a cove. He had shut the door quickly. He had not seen the inn (which was not visible from the doorway of the shed), and he had no idea anymore whether it, or even he himself, had ever existed.

Now, Mr. Cervantes had raped an awful lot of people in his day, two of them his sisters, and consequently all he had been able to think when Mr. Briscoe came at him was that he was finally, in a manner of speaking, getting his in the end. Since he could not remember anything after starting down the stairs in the hotel, it occurred convincingly to him that he was dead and in hell, buggered by the Devil. Mr. Cervantes would have struggled violently against any human rapist, but that had not seemed to be the case in the workshed. Even when Mr. Briscoe untied him, Mr. Cervantes, listening to the sound, outside the fragile structure, of what seemed the destruction of the entire universe, had merely lain terrified on the floor and watched the monster, muttering unintelligibly, depart into the storm.

Mr. Cervantes had no way to figure any of it out. His head hurt terribly, and now his bum hurt, too, and he certainly had no intention of leaving the shed. It was, at least, warm. Unfortunately he had not sat there ten minutes before the wind tore the roof off. Seawater began gurgling up through the floorboards, and finally the shed started to come apart as if it were being struck repeatedly by a gigantic baseball bat. The door blew off its hinges, and Mr. Cervantes stared openmouthed into a maelstrom of approaching secondary surf, boiling over the wreckage of the breakwater.

"Chíngame!" Mr. Cervantes said, with great emotion (an unfortunate phrase), and held on crying to a leg of the workbench. Two seconds later the shed exploded into matchwood, and sent Mr. Cervantes spinning into what appeared to be eternity, along with all of Mr. Briscoe's power tools.

Les Demoiselles d'Avignon

Georges felt awful about having lost a wing of his unin-sured inn, four guests, and two casuals, but there was nothing particularly to be done about it, and furthermore he was going to be a millionaire. It was really quite exciting as a new beginning, and even better as an end. He went up-stairs to see Simone. Previously, he had considered getting the Treatment, but that moment had passed, really: George put the strangely tractable and huge-eyed Simone against the wall with heroic abandon.

"God, I love the sea," he said a while later. "Do you like the sea?"

"I don't like anything I don't get paid for," said Si-mone, employing a towel.

"What a horrible philosophy."

"No it isn't," said Simone. She was so sick of hearing that from people.

George was perplexed. "What do you do after you get paid? I mean, what is the object of getting paid?"

"I like," she said, "to sleep."

She was not much of one for straight sex, and that, after George had come into the room, was exactly what she had been subjected to. Scowling, she lit a cigarette, wearing a pink nightgown that excited George immeasurably. He hadn't had enough money to pay her, until he had gone and looked into Norman's Woe. Now he had not only a very great deal of money, but also a machine pistol, a Swedish hand grenade, a Rolex Oyster, and a pair of handmade loafers.

"Well, let me tell you about my philosophy of life," said George.

Simone covered her ears.

"In my case it's a matter of realizing that nothing matters. I shouldn't call it nihilism, however, because when I think of a nihilist I think of sort of a grumpy fat girl with a horrible personal life who's found astrology transparent."

"There's one of those inside everybody, trying to get out," said Simone, who had actually been listening.

George took a swig of rum and opened the casement window, and let the snow whirl in. He took up Mr. Castro's Uzi and fired an entire clip of ammunition out into the storm, spraying bullets everywhere in prolonged bursts, pausing intermittently to scream, "I'm going to run tours in the Lake District! Fuck you!" Shells tinkled all over the room.

What George couldn't know was that his first shot blew off César Pilosi's hat, as César Pilosi crept toward the inn with a shotgun, and that Pilosi, considering his contract thereby negated (he had a strict no-shooting clause), began to run wildly away, only to catch fifteen in the back as he tried to get into his car.

The thing about life, George thought, was that just when you thought you were done, it was then that you became a millionaire with a machine gun. George belched, threw the machine gun out the window, then fell over and passed out.

The sound of the shouting and automatic fire caused, at various points in the house, Jesus Castro to briefly imagine that he was being rescued, Tim to pause terrified in the middle of the parlor, and Mr. Briscoe (who was sorting through Magdalene's closet, discarding clamdiggers, lamé sheaths, little black cocktail dresses, looking for something *perfect*) to fondly remember bayoneting Chinese soldiers on a Korean hill called Ice Cream Cone. Yes—fondly. Men don't admit it these days (what with all the enormously political vomiting in films when people get shot, and so forth), but the *scariest* thing about war for the average civilized man—like Mr. Briscoe—is how fucking enjoyable it is.

Post-traumatic stress disorder, in Mr. Briscoe's opinion, was a bunch of goddam bullshit. Mr. Briscoe often chuckled darkly at the idea of a nation of people who had to go into therapy whenever their lives failed to resemble television programs. Goddam reality's their problem, thought Mr. Briscoe, and adjusted his red shoe.

Chapter 39

Mr. Cervantes on Golgotha

Mr. Cervantes's reality consisted of doing forty knots over the bottom. Mr. Cervantes, torn by sharp rocks, nails, and broken lumber, cartwheeled along in the wave, the third that had sucked him sobbing toward the sea, and then flung him monstrously back. This time he fetched with a monumental collision on the beach. The broken wave retreated, full of wreckage, but without Mr. Cervantes, who managed to crawl sobbing partway up onshore, and to identify his location as a long ravine in the rocks, just before another wave came boiling in behind him, death-white, towering, blasting stones off the jetty, and pushing an acre of spume before it, as well as George's formerly sunken sloop, the *Anglia*, which came spinning drunkenly and horribly up from the deep—hideous, rotted, disintegrating, covered in barnacles and weeds, but heading straight toward the shore of the cove—and Mr. Cervantes—at nearly sixty knots.

Mr. Cervantes, whelmed to the neck by the dirty precedent foam, covered his eyes and emitted a high-pitched shriek. The wave hit the face of the littoral rocks, the *Anglia* jammed in the mouth of the ravine, her mast toppling and the hull exploding, and then the water, blasting into the chasm, hit Mr. Cervantes. According to the physics of the matter, Mr. Cervantes being in a natural funnel of rock, with an outlet higher than the entrance, and he being hit with the marine equivalent of the shock following an atomic explosion, Mr. Cervantes, a fraction of an instant later, shot from the far end of the chasm like a clown from a circus cannon.

He tumbled flailing nearly forty feet through the air, and landed flat on his back on the moor, momentarily out of the reach of the sea. "Fuck you," he shouted at the Atlantic, and wasted no time rising to his feet and getting further inland, scrambling over rocks and frozen blueberry bushes. He fell to his knees on a concrete slab beside an old snowdrifted barbecue, adjacent to the inn drive, and there thanked God in Spanish, his clothes torn, one yellow shoe gone, and the cord of a block sander wrapped tightly around his neck. Mr. Cervantes struggled with the power tool. An instant later this district was ten feet underwater.

Mr. Cervantes surfed and tumbled another twenty yards inland, flew over a small hill, and ended up in a cataracted river of seawater and melting snow, about five feet deep, which was flooding down the lower part of the driveway. He grabbed a lamppole, and hanging to it, weeping, saw his own rented car and a wrecked Volvo carried off down the driveway, and tumble one after the other off the edge of the promontory, the Volvo's lights still on, raking upward through the snow. Something grabbed at Mr. Cervantes's jacket and he shrieked and batted at it. He saw a ghastly white face staring at him, round of eye and mouth. César Pilosi had walked seven miles to the hotel after his car went off the road, only to be shot to pieces, and now drowned in a driveway. He gave up the ghost, floated slowly away, and went over the edge of the headland like a dead salmon over a dam.

The inn itself was above, and relatively intact, looking as noble and inviolable as Mont-St.-Michel, its apex of rock become an island. The great seas divided on the northeastern rocks of the promontory, and exploded harmlessly, roof-high, and higher, on either side of the Admiral Benbow. Mr. Cervantes realized that the inn was definitely the place to be, and after a surge containing smashed lawn chairs and a picnic table went past and subsided, he splashed up the driveway and staggered in the front door. Unable to cope with anything (the sight of Tim Picasso walking around in circles Hamlet-like while holding a machine gun was not encouraging), he ducked into the lobby closet and pulled the door shut behind him, wishing for all the world that he were in Florida.

Chapter 40

"Why Art?" Asked Doris

There was no way whatsoever to get out of the hotel, what with the causeway underwater, and with Mr. Castro hog-tied in the dining room there was nothing for Tim to do personally, and so toward dawn—it having been a night of some energy expenditure—while everyone in the hotel slept, the snow stopped falling, and the wind fell off dramatically. The nor'easter still blew in window-rattling gusts of up to gale force, but these became less frequent, and with the running of the tide, the storm surge collapsed and the seas diminished, as the black clouds of the storm boiled away to the south. In the east, the sky gradually became lucent, a nacreous overcast, rose-tinged, beyond the black scape of the lighthouse island. Gulls took tentatively to the air.

The coast road had been blown away mainly in horrible chunks, and was covered with boulders, and most of the houses along the coast had been flattened. But the Admiral Benbow, though lacking its billiards room, stood proudly intact so far as anyone observing from the coast road might have determined. In the cove below the hotel, Mr. Briscoe's lobster boat was still gamely afloat, though it was half full of water, part of the front deck was gone, and the windows of the pilothouse were smashed. Its automatic bilge pumps were working, though, and the boat rode, each minute that passed, incrementally higher in the water.

Inside the inn, the propane heat still plugged away as well as it ever did (which at the best of times wasn't very), and George, intensely hungover, but only partly ashamed of himself, was making bacon and eggs on the propane range, by the light of an oil lamp hung from a hook. Simone was upstairs in George's bed; Magdalene had just gotten out of Tim's bed, where she had waited for him all night in vain (he had passed out drunk on the parlor sofa, clutching a machine gun). Magdalene went glumly along the hall, holding a candle, to see if the hot water was working—which it amazingly was. Mr. Briscoe had just woken up from a satisfactory dream in which he served with distinction at

Bunker Hill (Oh! Had he only been able to save Dr. War-
ren!), and was eating four of the Percodans the doctor over
to Essex give him for his back. Come in handy, thought Mr.
Briscoe, when your arm's broke—though even Mr. Briscoe
was aware, ever since one of his ears had come off, that the
broken arm was the least of his worries . . . if a man in his
position could be said to have any worries at all. Tim had
slept nearly eight hours on the sofa by the fire, and he woke
feeling great. He experienced a guilty shock, though, when
he saw that the shed in which he had placed Mr. Cervantes
had disappeared—so now he was trying to be kind to Jesus
Castro, who was still hog-tied in the dining room. Mr. Cervantes, unbeknownst to anyone, was asleep under a pile of
coats in the lobby closet, dreaming of windmills.

"I gotta change my pants," said Jesus Castro.

"Well. I don't know if I can allow that," said Tim, whose
hair was sticking up remarkably, "but I am going to put
these handcuffs on you"—he had obtained them from upstairs—"which ought to be better than the speaker wire."

"No shit," said Jesus Castro.

"Then you can have some bacon and eggs."

Jesus Castro looked at Tim as if bacon and eggs were
not terrifically high on his agenda—but on the other hand,
he was hungry.

"I'm sorry about all of this," said Tim seriously. "In
many ways you were very good to me, and there is an argument that I shouldn't have stolen your money. But at the
same time I had a distinct impression that when you came
to get the money in Boston, you'd kill me, and take back
even what you'd already paid me."

Jesus Castro bit his lip, and wondered whether he was

always so transparent. He submitted to handcuffs, Simone's special pair, while Tim held the Beretta to his head with one hand and clicked the handcuffs with the other. Tim then padlocked a length of chain to the handcuffs, cut the speaker wire that bound Mr. Castro's ankles, stood up on the table, the pistol trained on Mr. Castro, and padlocked the other end of the chain to the stem of the chandelier. Mr. Castro (who looked pretty well used to this sort of thing) sat down grumpily at the table, smelling of urine.

Tim, after snipping away the speaker wire, poured Mr. Castro some coffee, and sat down on the other side of the table.

"We've decided what to do," said Tim.

"Good for you," said Jesus. "So have I."

"Frankly," said Tim, nervously ignoring this, "there are so many casualties already that we're just going to leave, and let people assume that George and Magdalene were killed in the destruction of the billiards room. We'll leave you here, with heat, food within reach. Sooner or later someone will find you. Probably the police. What do you think of that?"

"What I supposed to thing?" asked Jesus Castro.

"It's better than killing you."

Jesus Castro seemed to think it a matter of insignificant degree.

"I'm sorry."

"You win some, some tine, and you some the other tine lose some—maybe," said Jesus Castro.

George came in with a tray of bacon and eggs. "Good morning, Mr. Wassermann."

"I am Jesus," said Jesus.

"Awfully sorry about all this."

"Don' worry aboud," said Jesus Castro. He began to eat bacon and eggs, manipulating the fork awkwardly with his manacled hands. It was far from the ideal situation, to be sure, but absolutely the worst thing that could happen would be that he would take the Fifth, fly in his lawyers, get out on bail, have the witnesses killed, bribe the police, and if worst came to worst, blow up the DA with a car bomb and continue as before in Miami. It would be troublesome and expensive, but sometimes business was good, and sometimes business was bad. Jesus Castro chewed bacon, and smiled self-deprecatingly at Tim, imagining the day when that earnest young head would arrive at his feet in a bowling bag. He cheered up slightly.

Tim accompanied George back into the kitchen.

"Half in cash, half in securities. And the minute the road's plowed we're out of here. Or if Mr. Briscoe dies, we could run his lobster boat to Boston. We're all dead. Do you mind being dead and in Canada?"

"I've been dead for years," said George, "and I might as well have been in Canada. But I still haven't gotten it straight in my head. Let me go through it one more time. Plan B. The not-dead plan. Situation B: the police come and find us, and it's all 'Oh, what happened at your inn?'"

Tim rolled his hand: pray continue.

"You were never here," said George, "as at the appearance of the police you will jump out the window."

"Right."

"The only other guest besides the late Fiction Workshoppers and Mr. Castro was a Latin man wearing yellow shoes, whom, at the height of the storm, Mr. Castro overpowered, beat about the head, and threw into the cove, tied with clothesline and gagged with duct tape."

"Yes. Poor bastard was in the shed. The body may wash up."

"I understand," said George, brightly, washing dishes.

"And then the instant Jesus Castro is arrested," said Tim, "you get the fuck out of the country."

"Oh, yes. And if they start asking too many questions, I'll feign insanity, probably something along the lines of post-traumatic stress disorder."

"Excellent."

"And I'll be believed, because on top of everything else, my wife left me after having had sex with another man in a hot-tub establishment."

"Right."

"God, it works," said George. "Urethra."

"Urethra?"

"Eureka. Oh, I don't know. Whatever it was that Marat said in the bath." George smashed a glass.

"Mr. Castro being Mr. Castro," said Tim, ". . . I mean, look at him . . . you won't be asked too many questions. He threatened to kill you because you saw him kill the man with yellow shoes, but you managed to hit him over the head with the fireplace poker while he was eating Chinese food, and secured him with handcuffs and chain."

"Which I happen to have on the premises because my wife was an adulterous masochist."

"Exactly. Now, after driving Simone and Magdalene to Boston, I will wipe the car clean of fingerprints, and leave it in a very bad Hispanic section of town, with the keys in the ignition."

"It's genius," said George.

"Fiction is what makes sense in a courtroom. Never forget that. Reality doesn't."

Tim went along the passage, and happily up the stairs to see about either paying off or suffocating Mr. Briscoe, and disappeared from view just as Mr. Cervantes emerged groggily from the lobby closet. Mr. Cervantes looked terrible. He was covered with dried salt and spume, which residue whitened his skin and wrecked clothes, and his hair stood up coarsely, making him look like a man in a cartoon who has seen a ghost. The lavender sock was half off his one shoeless foot, he was a mass of cuts, scrapes, and bruises, and he still had no real idea what had happened, whether he was alive, or where he was. His last reasonable memory was of exactly this hallway. He smelled bacon, and limped toward the source of the smell.

"Jefe," said Mr. Cervantes.

"Now we do business," said Jesus Castro.

Chapter 41

I Don't Care Anymore

In the shower, at the end of the upstairs hall, Magdalene was soaping Simone's back. She had rather mixed feelings about it, which is to say that she was tremendously aroused, and totally unable to admit it. Simone, not surprisingly, had no such delicacy. She turned around slowly, with an ironic stare from her cornflower eyes, and after an interval of profound empathy, kissed Magdalene on the mouth.

"Oh my God," said Magdalene. At that moment there was a blast of celestial light and what appeared to be a canoe, containing several periwigged scientists, one of them screaming, "Sic omnia designantur," shot through one wall and discharged through the opposite wall.

"What the fuck was that?" asked Simone disinterestedly.

"I never expected this," Magdalene said. "I mean, lesbianism isn't something you expect to leap at you out of an alley, like a writer is getting drunk, and has lost control of his characters."

Simone sat cross-legged on the bathroom floor, smoking a cigarette, and said nothing.

"I mean, I *loved* men until about fifteen minutes ago, except for the tall woman at the frame shop, and now I want nothing to do with them at all. How did this happen?"

"You got in the shower with me."

"No, you got into the shower with *me*."

"Same difference," said Simone.

"I remember thinking, Why is she getting into the shower with me? and I remember thinking, Why don't I mind that she's getting in the shower with me? After you put on the sponge mitten, of course, I didn't think anything at all."

"You want a butt?" asked Simone.

"Yes, I think I do."

"Nice tits," said Simone.

"Do you think so, really?"

"Yeah."

"Thank you very much."

Simone, her back to the hamper, exhaled smoke, and looked critically at the universe.

"Obviously I can't go with Tim," Magdalene said. "I know it will hurt him."

"No it won't," said Simone.

"Of course it will."

"No it won't," said Simone. "That's the only reason you think it's a dilemma. If it would hurt him you'd have no indecision at all."

"What an awful thing to say," said Magdalene.

"It's true," said Simone, shortly, and flicked her cigarette butt into the toilet bowl. "Look, I've been here for two days. You think I don't know how you operate?"

Magdalene frowned. Instead of saying, "I'm confused," as she was really tempted to do, she said:

"Life is very complicated."

"No it isn't," said Simone. "It's just always the reverse of whatever people are trying to say it is."

"What do you mean?"

"I don't know. I don't know why I said that. I had this sort of weird feeling, and then it came out of me like a cartoon bubble." There was a pause.

"Rose the teaching assistant was severely overworked," said Simone.

"No sooner had she criticized the politics of one story than there was another which had to be vetted. It's a good thing," added Magdalene happily, "that she hadn't to check the grammar and spelling as well!"

"Hmmm," said Simone.

"There was a knock on the door of Dr. Locarno's office," said Magdalene. "Rose, a sneer on her carbuncled face, slowly crutched over to the door through the thick atmosphere of omniscient third person."

"Whatever," said Simone.

Chapter 42

Venus Rising

Mr. Briscoe opened the door of George and Magdalene's room and emerged wearing Magdalene's wedding gown, a tiara, a fox stole with glass eyes in the stuffed head, and of course, his single red evening shoe.

Tim, who had just reached the top of the stairs, stopped and stared.

"Good morning, sir," he said.

"My lungs are fillin' up. I know gangrene when I see it." Mr. Briscoe, tiara askew, hacked, gagged, ejected a clam. "Yeah, I was in the goddam water too long. I'm up against it this time. This is how I wanna go, son. It don't mean nothin' dirty."

Tim heard a thud, and something between a whine and a sob, from the bathroom, where the shower was running. Tim wondered what Magdalene could be doing in there.

"It's very attractive, Mr. Briscoe. Your attire."

"I'm gonna tell that son of a bitch runs this place to have 'em lay me out in this wedding dress. And I don't want nothing expensive, get me? They ask an arm and a leg for them caskets. I won't pay it. I want a plain box and a plain hole and a Congregational service. Flowers I don't mind. I want a headstone that reads, 'Ed Briscoe, he had his vision.' What I don't want is no ambulance."

"I wouldn't think of it," said Tim.

"Yeah, I'm done for, said Mr. Briscoe. "Called to goddam Glory. Son of a bitch."

"I don't know if you want to go downstairs."

"Get the hell away from me. I'm a dead man, son, I'm going home, and I just want to walk around awhile in this red shoe."

Tim realized that it hardly mattered at all. Mr. Briscoe started carefully down the stairs, coughing and dragging great wheezing breaths of air. His tiara fell off, and he felt at his head, but continued on his way. Tim started to rap on the bathroom door, where the shower was still audibly running, but decided against it, and went along to attend to his packing and to count out George's three-quarter million dollars.

Downstairs in the kitchen, George was just finishing up the dishes. He paused to gaze out the window at the lighthouse. A moment later he realized, after a flash of insignificant pain, that a French knife was pinning his yellow-gloved hand to the wooden drainboard. He tried to move his hand and could not.

"Oh dear," said George.

"Fucking guy," said Jesus Castro, and whacked George disgustedly. George's mortarboard flew off and he pitched face-first into the dishwater, in which Mr. Cervantes undertook to drown him, while Mr. Castro made certain observations of the present situation.

Chapter 43

Actual Modern Fiction

Yes, Mr. Briscoe was certainly up against it, but by the time he had figured out exactly how he was going to depart this world for paradise—it came to him with a bang—the Percodans had kicked in nicely, and he felt like a million bucks. He limped elegantly into the parlor and had himself a breakfast whiskey, ignoring the big spic or guinea or what have you who was staring openmouthed at him from the dining room doorway.

"That's right, go ahead and look," said Mr. Briscoe. "Get your goddam eyes full, you spaghetti-bending son of a bitch. I'm going to God, and I want to be properly dressed."

"Who these fuck are you?" asked Jesus Castro politely.

"That little feller standing there with you sure as hell knows who I am, don't you, boy. Well, if you come back for seconds, I'm afraid I can't oblige you. I got this gangrene from being in the water, and my arm's broke." Mr. Briscoe took a belt of whiskey.

"Fucking maricón—"

"It wasn't exactly what I thought it would be. If I had it to do over again, all things being equal, which they ain't, I'd ask God for a man I could connect with on some emotional level, like Lev'rett Purdy, over to Janesville. I don't expect you know Lev'rett, but he's a roofer, with a solid business, and him and I, in a better world, could have gone through life together. Very attractive gentleman. Favors overalls. Only thing wrong with the son of a bitch is he buys Japanese, and don't I give him hell for it. You boys want a drink?"

"Jefe, este es el hombre que me chingó en mi culo," said Mr. Cervantes, in tears, and Jesus Castro looked at Mr. Briscoe with wide eyes.

"I don't speak Italian, son—"

"¡Español!"

"—and I don't like the sound of it. Circumstances being different, I might keep my mouth shut about that, but I'm on my way out of this vale of troubles, and with that in mind, I'll tell you that I don't like guineas, never have, and I don't give a good goddam who knows it."

"Shut up you fucking maricón."

"Macaroni my ass," muttered Mr. Briscoe, and limped out of the room with his glass of whiskey. Mr. Cervantes started to whirl at him, in tears, but Jesus Castro caught him by the back of the coat, and slapped him.

"What the fuck's wrong wit' you?"

"Este hombre en el vestido de matrimonio me chingó en mi culo."

"¿Qué? ¿Qué?"

"He is the one who fucked me up the ass. It is the Devil."

"Wait a ming. Don' make no noise. You see we got any guns? You ask yourself maybe, who got the guns? You thing maybe, you don' got no guns, somebody else got the guns, maybe you be quiet?"

"That man in the dress fucked me up the ass."

"So what. You thing later he be hard to find? What's wrong wit' you? I try to teach you good. Listen. We go to burn this fucking place down. You go side, take a hose, get me some gasoline from the car. Okay? Can you do these for me?"

Mr. Cervantes nodded, in tears. "Por favor—jefe—por favor, mira— Este hombre en el vestido de matrimonio mi chingó en mi culo . . ."

"You get me the gas, then later I let you kill the old man in the dress. As a favor from me, to you."

Just at that moment, Jesus Castro noticed that, of all the things he didn't expect, his Uzi was in plain view on the parlor mantelpiece.

"Jesus Christ," said Jesus Castro. "How aboud. Go get the gas. I check the phone still don't work."

Mr. Cervantes went, in tears, out the front door. Jesus Castro tried the phone at the desk, and then the one in the English phone box. Both were dead. He suddenly remembered that he had purchased the red telephone booth. If he burned down the hotel, so much for the booth.

"Aw, fuck," said Jesus Castro. He worked the door dolefully. "Is nice piss a shit."

But business contained many reversals. Hearing a movement above, Mr. Castro slipped into the lobby closet, and through a gap of an inch between the door and the jamb, he saw Tim Picasso descend the stairs, dressed in an overcoat and carrying a cracked leather duffel. He walked confidently through the door into the parlor, headed for the dining room. Jesus Castro crept out of the closet, and came up behind just as Tim stood staring openmouthed at the handcuffs discarded on the dining room table.

Fucking A, thought Jesus Castro. He snapped the action on the Uzi, and shouted, "Chinga tu madre you fucking maricón money thief bastard," which, in Mr. Castro's opinion, just about summed it up, except for the part where he slammed Tim's head repeatedly into the table. He pulled Tim upright and jammed the machine pistol underneath his chin.

"You gonna steal money from me again?"

"Evidently not," said Tim.

"Fucking A," said Jesus Castro.

Chapter 44

Mr. Briscoe Takes the Air

M r. Briscoe, limping down to the cove, had decided on dynamite. His wedding gown and the ends of his stole were flying in the wind. When he got to the dock, the first thing he noticed was that the dock didn't exist.

"I'll be goddamned," said Mr. Briscoe.

His lobster boat was still afloat, unlike the homemade piece of shit that had sunk on him out to the lighthouse; but how he was going to get out to the boat was quite a problem. He stood there in the wind for a while, brooding on the loss of shed, tools, lumber, skiff, all. Although he was obviously done for, he still hated to see good money go down the toilet like that, much less all of his American-made power tools, which had cost a pretty penny, and furthermore had great sentimental value. But what was gone was gone was gone, thought Mr. Briscoe sensibly, like the New Englander he was. At that moment he remembered that that asshole George Hawthorne had one of them Sunfishes up in the weeds beside the inn.

If Mr. Briscoe could drag or push that little fiberglass piece of shit down to the cove, then he could float across to his lobster boat (the *Aphros*) pretty as a bug on a wood chip, then fire up the old bitch, and probably, he estimated, have a thirty-to-forty-percent chance of making it out to the island alive—there to kneel, recommend himself to Almighty

God, and blow himself to Jesus with the fifty pounds of prime American dynamite he had in the blasting shed.

He hobbled uphill for the Sunfish, and happened to see the little faggot with one yellow shoe apparently trying to steal the hubcaps or something from a sharp-looking Kraut automobile. Mr. Briscoe didn't like to see anything like that, but in his opinion, people who bought foreign deserved what they got, and furthermore, he had his own business to attend to, and if everyone could say that, the world would so clearly be a better place that there was in fact no argument. Mr. Briscoe wanted to wear a wedding dress and blow himself up with dynamite. If someone else wanted a German automobile, they could mind their own goddam hubcaps.

He ignored the boy, and attended to business. Still, he found it impossible to budge the Sunfish by himself. When it occurred to him to ask the boy to lend him a hand, he could no longer see him. Mr. Briscoe went along the side of the hotel and looked in through the kitchen window. He saw a knife sticking through a yellow-rubber-gloved human hand on the counter, but not much else. He limped along looking for a stick or something he could use as a pry-bar to knock the Sunfish on its way down to the cove, when he remembered that what he had seen in the kitchen was a knife sticking through a human hand. Mr. Briscoe fretted. He was busy as hell at the moment, but obviously he had to go and investigate.

"I am what I say I am," said Mr. Briscoe. "I am the Eggman."

Chapter 45

A Mirror Very Necessary

Y ou thing is funny you steal my money?"

"The way you say it is funny."

"What the fuck you thing aboud it now?" asked Jesus Castro, sticking the Uzi beneath Tim's chin again.

"Perhaps you could tell me what I'm supposed to think."

"You suppose to thing it ain' funny at all. You got my money in this bag?"

"Yes. Most of it. Where's George?"

"Fucking guy do the dish and talk to himself in the kitchen. I don' wanna hurt nobody, but I have to hit the guy on the head. You know aboud hit people on head, don' you."

"Sorry."

"Hey, don' take it so bad. You win some, then you lose some, and you know what I min. I tell you what I'm gonna do. I no gonna shoot you, these tine. What I'm gonna do is fucking artistic."

"Great," said Tim.

"This is what I'm gonna do. I'm gonna tie every body up in the natural position, you unnerstan' me? One inna chair, other one on top of the other one inna bed, one here, one there, one sit nice at the table, and then I burn down the whole fucking place, you follow me?"

"I'm afraid I do, yes."

"You gonna steal more money belongs to me?"

"Apparently, no."

"Fucking right," said Jesus Castro.

Tim felt compelled to explain himself.

"You should understand that I never stole anything in my life before I took your million and a half dollars. It was completely out of character. And obviously I'm *very sorry for it*."

"You do pretty good. You win some, you lose some. Lemme tell you some things today some time. What you can' do in business is let no one have second chance. What you should do with me you got me tie up on the floor? Bang. That's what you do. That way, you would not be in this position, you know what I min."

"Yeah. I suppose I do."

"Too bad. Smart kid. Good-lookin' kid. Don't get me wrong. I ain' no maricón. But you and me coulda do some thing together, maybe go to Mexico, week end, eat some shrimp. Too late for that. Put the bag down the floor, keep your hands on top your head."

"Simultaneously?"

"You figure it out."

Mr. Cervantes came in with a rusted can of gasoline, his face blotchy from the cold, smoking a cigar. "That car's a fuckin' diesel, boss. I fine this in the garage. Hey. Is the guy."

"No shit," said Jesus Castro. "Is a guy. What you thing I am? No good at this?"

"Fuck you," Mr. Cervantes shouted in Tim's face.

"Don' do that, I take care of it already," said Mr. Castro. "Go in the kitchen, get me some candles and paper cups."

"¿Qué?"

"¡Candelas y copas de papel!"

"Candelas and paper copas?"

"Sí. Pronto."

"Interesting word, 'pronto,'" said Tim. "I was shocked to find it was the way Italians answer the telephone. I always feel that they haven't enough time to listen to what I have to say."

"Language funny thing," said Jesus Castro. "Your romantic languages especialmente."

"It's rather funny to think that I was called the unnatural heir to the Romantic tradition," said Tim. "I suppose it doesn't matter now."

"No," said Jesus Castro, and lit a cigar.

Chapter 46

And Yet Their Labors Lost

In the kitchen, George, like a twisted, one-point Christ, was in a peculiar, almost votive attitude, with his soaked head against the cabinets and his legs curled beneath him. He was breathing. He was also dreaming. In his dream he was wearing gumboots and a tweed shooting jacket, and being completely ignored by both publican and besotted yokels in an English country pub. For some reason this filled him, in the dream, with visionary rapture. Mr. Cervantes, thinking George dead, simply stepped over him and looked through more cabinets. He failed to see Mr. Briscoe's gray head pass by the window. Candelas, they were all over the place. Copas de papel were a different fucking story. He even pulled the French knife out of George's hand and shifted the body so that he could look in the cabinets under the sink. No luck. Finally he found some paper cups in the pantry, and went back out to the parlor with them.

"Jefe, mira."

"What you wan', a fucking medal? Gimme those. You take this gun and don' let this guy move."

"Sí."

"You shoot this guy, and I never respect you no more," said Mr. Castro very seriously, in a scene written in 1991 and published serially with cult success in 1994 without winning anything the way some people apparently did with it.

Tim was left with Mr. Cervantes. Jesus Castro took the candles, paper cups, and gasoline, and smoking a cigar, went happily down into the cellar, amidst the boilers and horrible machines. After reconnoitering the place, which had an old-fashioned fuse box and nearly prehistoric wiring, he decided that it would be best to go for the short-circuit effect. He filled one of the paper cups with gasoline and put it into the fuse box. He stuck a candle in the paper cup and lit the wick. As the soft light lit his face, he smiled. Immediately the denouement had a time element.

Jesus Castro liked deadlines, personally. He felt that

pressure—that is, not having the time to do anything but be a genius—was salubrious, and brought out the best in an Artist, separated the artist from the artifex, art from artifexion (or higher artifexion from lower artifexion, for that matter, though Jesus had never thought about it), and no one could tell him any differently.

He set two more incendiary devices, near electrical relays, and went back upstairs. Magdalene and Simone were now sitting together on the sofa, both in their overcoats and with their suitcases, and they looked very upset indeed.

"I get you two more, boss!" said Mr. Cervantes.

Tim sat beside them. Mr. Cervantes, who was covering them all with the machine pistol, and had periodically been gripping his own genitals, was very pleased with himself, and indicated the women, at whom he made kissing noises, by way of psychologically recovering from being sodomized.

"I don't want to hurt no body," said Jesus Castro, taking the machine pistol from Mr. Cervantes, whose face fell, as if he had lost an erection. "But I gotta kill you all."

Nobody said anything.

"Some time business go that way, you know what I min. Okay, you." He pointed at Tim. "You stand up. Hey wait a ming. Why your hand in your pocket?"

"It isn't."

"It is too fuck the pocket. Take the hand out or I kill you."

Tim removed his hand from his pocket. It had taken him ten minutes to get his hand into the pocket. He stood up, dejectedly. Mr. Castro crossed to him, patted the coat, and smiled delightedly. He pulled out the Beretta.

"Hey, you got this all the time?"

"Yes," said Tim.

"Why don' you use it? What a fucking asshole." Mr. Castro laughed. Mr. Cervantes laughed. "What a fucking asshole," repeated Mr. Castro. "Him have this fucking gun all the tine." It was really very funny. Even Tim smiled, and shrugged. Jesus Castro, in a very good mood, tossed the pistol cinematically to Mr. Cervantes, who, still laughing, caught it deftly. No one expected it to go off, but it did, very loudly. Mr. Cervantes, looking confused, fell down with a hole in the middle of his forehead. All their ears were ringing as they stared down at Mr. Cervantes. One of his legs kicked, and then he didn't move at all. Mr. Castro's cigar fell out of his mouth.

"You go to be shit me," he said, unaware that Mr. Briscoe stood behind him. Mr. Briscoe hit Jesus Castro on the head with a framing hammer.

Chapter 47

Good-bye

I loved that boy," shouted Mr. Briscoe, emotionally, as the diesel of the lobster boat warmed up. "Never told him, but I loved him. That's a fact."

In his wind-whipped wedding dress, Mr. Briscoe stumped about the deck in his red shoe. Even in the cove the swell was sickening, and the horizon tilted, levitated, sank. Jesus Castro, handcuffed, two cinder blocks chained to his ankles, sat morosely on the wheelhouse floor, an unlit cigar in his mouth. Mr. Cervantes's body, wrapped in a blanket, was also draped in padlocked tire chains and weighted the same way.

"Terrible way for the poor little son of a bitch to go out," said Mr. Briscoe. "That spaghetti-cranking son of a bitch got his pistol-safety merit badge from the goddam I-talian army, I guess."

"Fuck you," said Jesus Castro.

Tim stood drinking whiskey with George, whose hand was wrapped in a mitten of bloodstained gauze. The women stood briefly waving onshore, then got into Mr. Castro's rented Mercedes and drove away.

"That's that," said George. "Strange that I don't mind if she leaves me for a woman. I would have left her for a woman if I'd met one. Of course I did meet a woman—but Magdalene left with her. I can't help thinking that life is very ordinary."

Mr. Briscoe gunned the throttle. Blue smoke ejac-
ulated into the wind. Tim went forward and cast off the
mooring line, and the lobster boat hammered out into the
Atlantic, rolling heavily, Mr. Briscoe at the controls, wearing his cap with earflaps along with the wedding dress, an
ensemble that had ceased to seem peculiar. Tim dropped
back into the cockpit. He was exhilarated by the act of going
to sea.

"If they didn't let people like that son of a bitch into the
country," said Mr. Briscoe, "we'd be a hell of a lot better off."

"I don't know if you can say that, Mr. Briscoe."

"Goddam bootlegger," said Mr. Briscoe, from his particular frame of reference.

"I am under privileged," said Mr. Castro experimen-
tally.

Tim squatted beside Mr. Castro.

"Are you warm enough, sir?"

"You got to be shit me. What you care if I warm enough?
You gonna put me in the water with cement fucking shoe,"
said Jesus Castro, who refused after this to say anything
else, and merely looked on dejectedly when, with great difficulty, because of the rolling and pitching of the boat, Mr.
Cervantes's body was rolled over the transom.

The lighthouse island leaped and wavered in the offing.

"It's impossible not to think about Virginia Woolf,"
George said.

"That's where you're wrong," said Tim.

"You'll have to speak for yourself. I'm absolutely terrified of her. I mean, she called James Joyce a queasy undergraduate. Christ. There goes the whole shooting match, if
you think about it."

They were very solemn for a moment.

"Do you think she ever got that room of her own?" asked George.

"Hang on, boys," shouted Mr. Briscoe. The lobster boat nearly pitchpoled. Spray cannoned overhead. George hung on to a rail. Unnoticed, Mr. Castro bleakly vomited.

"I'm done for, boys," shouted Mr. Briscoe. "Going to God."

"Yes," said George. "You've been saying that."

A little while later they threw Mr. Castro over the side, in one hundred fathoms of water, and the lobster boat pottered on under the lee of the island, and into the anchorage cove. The lighthouse, sharp in every dimension, stood against the overcast eastern sky. They landed on the island.

"I dislike phallic symbols," said Tim. "They make me nervous. It's insidious. Even when you don't see one, all of a sudden you see one, unnaturally, because someone else would."

"It's a new century, though," said George, "without you-know-who in it."

"Good."

"I'm done for, boys," said Mr. Briscoe, and headed up the path to the dynamite shed in his wedding dress and single red evening shoe. He disappeared inside. Tim sat down on a rock just above the jetty, the duffel of money on his knees. George, hunched in his wind-whipped overcoat, drinking whiskey, looked interestedly at his bandaged hand.

"I have a gift, right, granted," said Tim. "What am I supposed to do with my gift? Make a film? Write? I can write, too, you know. What should I do? Sit in a fucking room on an NEA grant and burn three pages on a description of lamplight and a cowboy eating beans? I'll tell you, George, if it comes to that, we might as well weave baskets. Or be dead."

"If art's not big enough, though," said George, "the only thing left is to become a god."

"Exactly," said Tim.

Strangely enough, at exactly that moment (Mr. Briscoe's eyes rolling back in his head as he crammed two crackling wires together), the lighthouse exploded. George and Tim were slammed to the ground. Both men looked disinterestedly around. Some pieces of the lighthouse and, Tim supposed, Mr. Briscoe, hung high in the air as if practicing a kind of delicacy about submitting to gravity, then plummeted smoking into the sea. There was no fire, and not much smoke. The air was primarily full of wildly disturbed gulls. An empty red evening shoe bounced on the ledge, and George hesitantly picked it up. It was smoldering.

"There reason is," said George, "and begins her reign."

"Whatever any of us do," said Tim, "none of us will ever do anything as good as that."

Tim immediately sat down on a rock. His ears were ringing. He looked around the island, and saw that among the mottoes on the rocks was painted this:

MORTE D'AUTHOR

Tim gazed again at the rubble of the lighthouse.

"He's been thinking about this for some time, George."

After a few moments, the gulls settled where they had

been, the pall of smoke broke up in the wind, and the island was as before, except that it didn't have a phallic symbol sticking out of it.

"Well, he certainly had his vision, anyway," said George, and uncapped the whiskey. "An artist. Look at that. Blow yourself up in a lighthouse with 'So' on it and you've more or less said it all."

"He was more than an artist, George."

"What?"

"Well. He was a transvestite accomplice in a homicide. It sounds grimly specific. But that's maybe what life is: a transit from the green vague promise of unforméd youth to . . . grotesque specificity."

"Why are you talking that way?"

"I have no idea." Tim took a pull of whiskey. "I'm a lot more specific than I used to be. I used to be rather amorphous. Now I'm an artist, a thief, an adulterer, and a cold-blooded murderer. You know, that's why they used to have so many saints. So you got something, no matter who you were. Like Christmas at the orphanage."

"I'm a failed innkeeper, a cuckold, and a revolting poet." George took the bottle back. "On the bright side, the only direction from here is up."

Tim drank whiskey, and stared toward land. "As far as the cops are concerned, you're also a probable arsonist. Your hotel's on fire," he said.

"Good," said George. "Can you run his boat?"

Tim could: it was his tragedy.

A half-mile across the water, ground swell and gull flight, the hotel burned strongly and brightly in the wind. No fire engines were yet in evidence anywhere on the disastrous coast. Tim led the way down over the icy rocks toward the dock, started the lobster boat, and ran it out of the cove. Right honorable, thought Tim (on behalf of Mr. Briscoe, probably). *I know not how I shall offend in dedicating my unpolished lines to your lordship, only if your Honor seem but pleased I shall I account myself highly praised, and vow to take advantage of all idle hours, till I have honored you with some graver labor. But if the first heir of my invention prove deformed, I leave it to your honorable survey and your honor to your heart's content, which I wish may always answer your own wish, and the world's hopeful expectation.* I divorce thee now in the Muslim form: Sayonara, sayonara, sayonara.

QUE SAIS-JE?
—A Frenchman

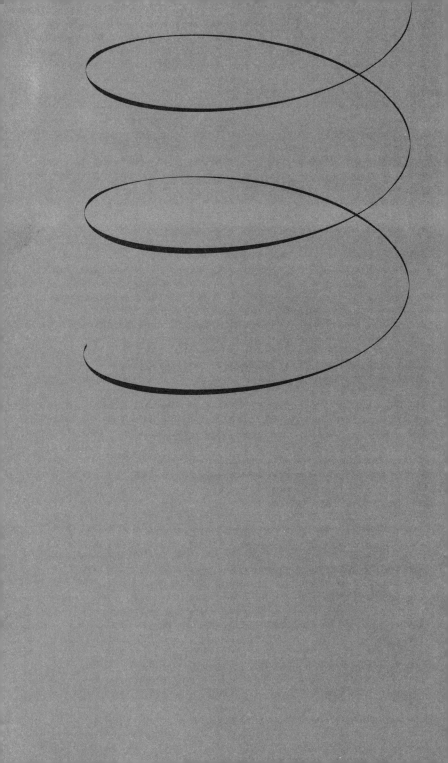